# WOLF
# JACKSON

Wolf Jackson

# WOLF JACKSON

## A Novel

# JORDAN FLOWERS

*Wolf Jackson* by Jordan Flowers
Copyright © 2019 by Jordan Flowers
All Rights Reserved.
ISBN: 978-1-59755-581-4

Published by:     ADVANTAGE BOOKS™
                  Longwood, Florida, USA
                  www.advbookstore.com

Library of Congress Catalog Number: 2019933648

First Printing: February 2020
20 21 22 23 24 25   10 9 8 7 6 5 4 3 2 1
Printed in the United States of America

# Table of Contents

ACKNOWLEDGMENTS.................................................................7

CHAPTER 1: THE LOST.............................................................9

CHAPTER 2: THE BROKEN .....................................................19

CHAPTER 3: THE SOUGHT OUT............................................23

CHAPTER 4: THE REGRETS ...................................................27

CHAPTER 5: THE SECRETS ....................................................29

CHAPTER 6: THE HURTS........................................................37

CHAPTER 7: THE JUDGED .....................................................45

CHAPTER 8: THE SHADOWS ..................................................53

CHAPTER 9: THE PROTECTED...............................................63

CHAPTER 10: THE WARNING.................................................69

CHAPTER 11: THE ASPECT ....................................................77

CHAPTER 12: THE INVASION ................................................87

CHAPTER 13: THE SCALPEL ..................................................91

CHAPTER 14: THE SECRET PAST.........................................101

CHAPTER 15: THE LOVED....................................................107

CHAPTER 16: THE RECKONING ..........................................111

CHAPTER 17" THE WOLF .....................................................121

CHAPTER 18: THE COLLIDE ................................................129

CHAPTER 19: THE JUSTIFIED...............................................139

CHAPTER 20: THE REDEEMED ...........................................145

CHAPTER 21: THE FOUND...................................................151

CHAPTER 22: THE HONORED..............................................155

CHAPTER 23: THE LIFE GIVEN ...........................................163

Wolf Jackson

# Acknowledgments

I want to thank a few people for making this dream happen. My amazing, God-fearing wife, Bailey, for being supportive of me during this process and encouraging me to make my dream come alive. Especially in the final stretch of the process, making this a perfect work before the Lord as it is worship through the gift He has given. My sister in the faith, Rachel Johnson, for reading over the very rough first draft ever seen by someone else and giving me the initial tools to create this masterpiece. My mother in the faith, Rebecca Borden, for all the hours she spent editing and tearing apart my third to last revision. My close friend and brother in Christ, Derek French, for editing the second to last revision and challenging me to honor God with my writing. Pastor Wayne Cordeiro, a man that I get to call both a mentor and a very good friend, for encouraging me to release my dreams and shoot for the stars, even when the world tells you that you will never make it. I would not have had the courage it took to release this story without your guidance. I also want to thank everyone else who believed in me and encouraged me along the way. It is your faith in the gift that God had given me that kept me striving to let this dream become a reality. For that, I am eternally grateful.

More importantly than all this, I thank my Father God in Heaven, my Savior and King, the Lord Jesus Christ, and the Holy Spirit who gave me the gift of writing to pull my life from the ashes and placed me before the Kingdom of Glory. Without You Lord, I would have never had this story in my heart. May it bring glory and honor to You and further Your Kingdom. In Your Holy and matchless Name. Amen.

# Chapter 1

# The Lost

Saturday, June 5th, 2013, 3 a.m., on the corner of Tremont and Park Avenue, Denver, Colorado. A shot rings out followed by seven more. The screech of tires as a car speeds down the road. People living in the neighborhood emerge from their homes to see what happened. They find a young man in his mid-thirties lying in the middle of the street, his dog tags glinting off the street lamps. One man approaches and finds the young man sprawled out in his own pool of blood. He feels for a pulse and finds none. "Call 9-1-1!!!" he screams to the bystanders. Five minutes later the authorities arrive and take the body away. His loved ones, if he had any, would be called later that morning.

9 a.m., same day, a man is awoken by his phone ringing. Switching it to speakerphone, he answers the call. A feminine voice fills the silence of the still room, asking, "Hello? William Jackson?"

"Yeah, who's this?" came his groggy response.

"I'm Detective Kate Westbrooke with the Denver Police Department; did I wake you?" the feminine voice asked.

"No, you're fine ma'am. How may I help you?" the man asked, his voice still groggy.

"Do you have a roommate by the name of Darnel Jones?" she asked.

"Yes, I do," the man responded hesitantly, "Is everything alright?"

"Well sir, I regret to inform you that we believe to have found him this morning. He was shot and killed around three o'clock on Park Avenue. Your number was labeled, 'In Case of Emergency,' in his cell phone. We need someone to come in and identify his body... Does Darnel have any living relatives that we may need to notify?" she replied.

The man sat there holding his phone with one hand and his head in the other. "Are you still there Mr. Jackson?" the woman asked.

"Yeah, yeah I'm uh… I'm here… Darnel didn't have any living relatives… just me..." he replied.

"Mr. Jackson, I understand that this must be very hard for you, but could you possibly make it in around noon today to identify Darnel?"

The man agreed and hung up the phone. Sitting at the edge of the bed he stared blankly into the mirror in front of him. When he realized where he was staring, he abruptly looked away.

The left half of his face was severely scarred from a burn that had long since healed. His ebony skin held bold contrast to the pale, ash-like scar tissue. The marred flesh began three inches behind his left ear, wrapping around the left side of his head, two inches above the ear. His ear was nearly gone, no longer holding the original shape, forming more of a bump that pressed to his head. Half of his left eyebrow had been replaced with crinkled flesh that wrapped around his left eye and down his jawline to his neck. The left side of his torso, his shoulder, upper back, peck, bicep, and hand were marred as well.

He was young, about twenty-seven years old. Despite his astronomical scar tissue, his body was in great physical condition. A set of silver dog tags with the words *Lieutenant William "Wolf" Jackson* etched into them, dangled close to his chiseled chest, clanging softly together as they swung back and forth gently on the chain. The man grasped them momentarily with his hand then released them so that they dangled motionless from his neck.

He sat silently in the stillness of the morning, refusing to move. The world seemed to crumble, making time and space feel nonexistent. His mind fought against the common denial everyone faces when they lose a loved one. Pain threatened to concave like an avalanche on his psyche as memories of his best friend challenged his resolve.

After what seemed like an eternity, his legs and arms began to feel less heavy, no longer hindering him from his ability to move. He wiped a bead of sweat from his bald head, stood up, and walked out of the room in a haze. A white bulldog followed close behind as he walked towards the kitchen. There he grabbed a bottle of water out of the refrigerator and walked into the bathroom to take a shower. Maybe the shower would wake him up from this nightmare. It didn't work: his best friend was dead.

Now fully clothed in tan cargo pants and a tight-fitting black hooded sweatshirt and black boots, Jackson sat on the couch in the front room. He scratched the head of his small, white companion. He looked at his service watch, 1100 hours, where had the time gone? He let out a deep sigh and once again battled for the strength to return to his limbs.

After a few minutes, he stood up and walked out the door, grabbing a green apple from the bowl on the coffee table on his way out, his small companion once again following close behind. Taking out his keys, he unlocked the lifted, black, 2005 Ford F150, SuperCrew Cab long bed in the driveway. He bent down to pick up his follower and gave a slight grunt at the dog's girth. Opening the driver side door with his free hand, he set the dog in the truck and waited for him to get into his designated space in the front passenger seat. Climbing in after the dog and taking his place behind the wheel, he shut the door and started the truck. The A/C kicked on and a guitar lick softly crackled out of the speakers as the smooth voice of Johnny Cash came to life. Wolf turned up the stereo from his steering wheel and put the big truck into reverse, pulling out of the driveway as the guitar retold the story of a man who had lost his way. Now his life is subject to the decisions he has made with no one left to blame but himself.

Wolf allowed the lyrics to fill his thoughts, sweeping away all his pain, at least momentarily. He let out a sigh, reached into his pocket, pulled out the apple and bit into it, put the truck in gear, and drove away from his three-bedroom house. After forty-five minutes of traffic, he finally reached the police station. "Stay in the truck Beef," he said as he exited the vehicle, tossing his apple core into a trash can a few feet away. Taking in a deep breath, he turned his face into a sheet of granite and walked into the station.

There was a flurry of voices blasting into his good ear as he entered the room. People were bustling about to different desks, taking calls, and rushing out the door to find yet another criminal. A blonde woman took him by the left arm and was making an attempt to ask questions. Annoyed, Wolf turned his head to the left so he could hear her out of his right ear. "Are you William Jackson?" she asked.

He recognized that voice: the woman on the phone from earlier that morning. He nodded his head and she led him into a small room with two chairs facing a desk with a high back chair. She motioned for him to have a seat in one of the two chairs in front of the desk, then sat herself in the high back chair, facing Wolf. There was a long pause as she began rifling through a folder. Wolf noticed her hair was pulled back in a hair tie to both keep it out of her face, as well as an attempt to hide that she had not washed or styled it that morning. Her pinstripe pant-suit was that of a professional, though it had been worn for at least twenty-four hours. She was a little frazzled; Wolf took note of her habit of overly fidgeting with her folder. The office had little to nothing on the walls except a plaque of recognition as *Detective of the Year*, inscribed with her name. Her stiff posture indicated a military background, perhaps infantry or naval. He noticed the cup of coffee sitting next to her hand; steam poured from the top. He could smell the black, dark brew from his seat five feet away: definitely navy.

The detective finally broke the silence, "Lieutenant, I'm sorry we have to meet on such circumstances. How are you feeling?"

Wolf held his stoic expression, "Been better, ma'am."

She nodded her head, "It's hard when you lose a good man..."

Wolf nodded his agreement. After another slight pause, Wolf was able to ask the question he knew he didn't want the answer to, "What happened?"

The detective once again took a long pause and opened the folder, turning it around so Wolf could read it. "Darnel was found on the corner of Tremont and Park Avenue at three o'clock this morning. He had been shot three times in the chest and once in the head. Witnesses said that they heard the gunshots, followed by the squealing of tires. One man made out what appeared to be an SUV fleeing the scene. We believe that the shooter pulled up alongside Darnel and shot him four times with a 9mm handgun, though at least six to eight were recorded fired by witnesses. No brass was found at the crime scene. Because of that, we believe that the shots were fired from inside the vehicle, more than likely from one of the passenger seats, based upon the trajectory of the bullets. By the time anybody got to Darnel, he was gone; there was no chance of saving him."

She stopped for a moment to clear her throat. Wolf sensed that she was feeling more emotions towards this case than she was letting on, "No one saw a license plate, and the traffic cameras did not catch anything due to a glitch in a system... which means—"

"You have no leads and it appears that someone may have been paid off to ensure that." Wolf interrupted her thought before she could finish it.

The detective looked down and nodded her head slightly. She lifted her head to look him in the eye; there was a fire-filled fury in her eye. "Off the record," she said in a little more hushed tone, "Those are my thoughts exactly. None of this adds up and there is too much evidence found inconclusive to be a random gang shooting. Even then, my supervisors are giving me only forty-eight hours to find evidence and put the culprit behind bars." Wolf began to take in the gravity of her words as she looked at him with tears forming in her eyes. "I am so sorry…" she said, then she buried her face in the folders once more.

Wolf felt a slight tremor try to form on his bottom lip, then quickly solidified his expression once again. Realization dawned in the forefront of his mind. He looked at the detective, raising his good eyebrow slightly. "What aren't you telling me?" he asked her sternly.

"I assure you, Lieutenant Jackson, there is nothing that I am hiding," she responded.

Wolf smirked slightly; he knew there was more to this. He wasn't going to rest until he knew the truth. "You refer to my brother as Darnel, yet you refer to me as Lieutenant Jackson. Either that is your way of honoring the dead, or you knew him… Judging from your posture I can tell that you served. Veterans wouldn't refer to another vet who has fallen without their rank unless they knew them personally. So, I will ask again, what aren't you telling me?"

"Darnel said you were quite the detective yourself," the detective responded. She let out a deep breath, then pulled another file out of her desk drawer. She opened the file so Wolf could read it. "Yes, I knew Darnel; he was an associate of mine. More than that, he was my friend. Our paths crossed about six months ago when he beat up a well-known drug dealer named Tyrone Simmons, also known as, 'The Aspect Enforcer,' or just, 'Aspect,' for short. Darnel caught some of his guys trying to sell drugs to kids by a church on the corner of 25th and Welton. He came in the next day to inform us about it. Unfortunately, due to his PTSD, my supervisor did not take him seriously and dismissed him. Said he was probably having a flashback and imagined the whole thing. However, being of a military background myself, I knew better.

"I have been trying to take Simmons down for two years now, but nothing sticks on him. I think he has some cops on payroll, which would explain the lack of evidence. Darnel was my informant/private investigator. He gave me intel and collected evidence. I thought he would be safe due to his background… I guess I was wrong…"

Wolf tried to gather his thoughts as he read through the file. "It says that Darnel was under a contract to work within the laws of this state, to only be an observant reporter, and to not interfere with police business." Wolf paused for a long moment, "So, basically what this is telling me is that you told him to win a war without ammunition for his rifle."

The detective took a long pause once again. "I am so sorry… I take complete blame for his death…"

Wolf could tell she meant her words. He felt an urge to comfort her, but that would crush his own resolve, which he would need for what he was about to ask for next. "May I see his body?" he asked.

The detective wiped the tears from her eyes and nodded her head. She led Wolf out of the room, down the hall, and into an elevator. Neither of them said a word as they descended to the bottom floor. The elevator opened, revealing another set of doors with the word *Coroner* written over them. Wolf followed the detective out of the elevator and through the double doors, into a cold, dingy room. Across from them was a wall covered with square metal cabinets. To the left of where they stood, a table was laid out in the middle of the room with a humanoid figure covered in a white sheet laying on top of it. There was an elderly man in the room; the detective walked over to him and whispered in his ear. The man shook his head, "He is not ready for viewing."

"He's ready," she said sternly. The man glared at her; then, seeming to back down, he walked over to the table and pulled back the sheet to reveal Darnel's body. "May we have the room?" the detective asked. The man grunted and left the room in a huff. She then looked at Wolf, "I hope this helps..." she said, and then cast her eyes towards Darnel.

Wolf stood there for what felt like an eternity. Once again his limbs felt like lead balloons. After a few moments, he built up his strength, walked towards his fallen friend, and placed his hand on the other man's forehead. With a blink of his eye, a single tear fell, splashing onto the dead man's cheek. Wolf abruptly stifled his emotions, choking down the tears, just for the moment. Though, he knew that he would not be able to for long. There was his brother, his friend, the only family he had left in this world, lying on a cold table in a poorly lit room. Silence filled the room as realization penetrated the resolve he fought so hard to control... Darnel was really dead. This was no dream, and he couldn't wake up from it.

"Darnel would have gone after that man without you. But he had a code of honor where he refused to work outside the rules. You didn't handicap him, he did that himself..." Wolf said to the detective in the hope to comfort her emotions.

"Thank you," she said, as she once again was wiping tears from her eyes. She handed him a bag containing a wallet, phone, keys, dog tags, and two rose gold rings attached to a small chain: one was a single, thick band, the other a dainty band with a teardrop ruby and a diamond halo. "Here are Darnel's personal effects; he would want you to have them," she told him.

Wolf took the bag from her. He opened it and pulled out the rings. He stared at the two rings for a moment then put them back in the bag. After a few minutes, they went back to the elevator. The doors closed and Wolf observed the bag in his hands, the dog tags glinting in the fluorescent light of the elevator. "I am not Darnel," he said after a long silence, "and I will not be signing any contract. You will get your evidence. Darnel will get justice. You have my word on that."

The detective looked up with grave concern as to what Wolf was saying. "You can't go after him. This is not Afghanistan and you aren't in a war-zone. There are laws; this is not the wild west!" she exclaimed.

"Don't worry about it, Detective. All I need you to do is stall your supervisor. Give me a week, and I will give you Simmons and his goons." Wolf stared at the detective, "Do you understand?"

She took a breath. "I can neither confirm nor deny I know what you are saying, because we are not having this conversation," she replied.

The elevator doors opened and Wolf exited the car. The detective put her hand on the door, keeping it open. "Off the record, make sure you scorch this monster. We can't take any chances." He looked back at the detective and nodded his head. He walked out of the police station and back to his truck. As usual, Beef was on the driver's side with his paws on the door, staring out the window waiting for his master. Wolf shook his head as the dog greeted him with *gruff* noises and snorts. He pursed his lips, letting out a quick shrill whistle. Beef tilted his head at him then returned to the passenger seat of the big truck and waited as his best friend climbed into the rig. Wolf sat heavily in the seat and patted the dog on the head. "You want a cheeseburger, Beef?" he asked. The dog started snorting in delight and wagging his tail excitedly. "Yeah, I knew you would," Wolf said as he started the truck and drove away from the police station.

Wolf Jackson

# Chapter 2

# The Broken

Four hours later: Wolf sat in the hall, his back resting on the pale white wall and his boots on the wooden door in front of him. He stared blankly at the grain in the wood, studying every detail. His left hand rested on his leg as his right hand rested on the cold metal of his Smith and Wesson M&P 45mm semi-automatic pistol, loaded and ready. Beef was sleeping next to his master's left leg with his little white head resting on his shin. A tear crept its way out of Wolf's eye, never to be seen by anyone else; he let it fall with a blink. The gun left the ground and was pressed firmly under his chin. Pain ripped through his psyche. His heart pounded in his ears, the dull rush of blood deafening in the silence. Tears flowed freely as the safety clicked off the gun. He grit his teeth and shut his eyes tightly. His hand shook as he tried to pull the trigger, but his body fought his mind, rendering his finger momentarily inoperable.

Wolf let out a loud roar as his arm shook violently trying to hold the gun in place. The gun went off with a loud crack, digging a hole in the wooden door of his brother's bedroom. More shots rang out as he emptied the ten-round magazine into the oak door. Beef jumped up with a start; after a brief pause, he let out an annoyed *gruff* and laid his head back down on his master's leg. The tears flowed hot down Wolf's cheeks now as the flood gates were finally opened. He screamed in anger and agony, then slung the weapon down the hallway.

He sat there for over an hour, weeping, before he finally had the strength to stand once more. Hesitantly, he reached out his hand and rested it on his brother's door. They had an agreement that they both respected. There were two areas neither of the two men were allowed to enter: one another's room and the master bedroom upstairs. Both Wolf and Darnel suffered from post-traumatic stress and their rooms were their own personal sanctuaries. The upstairs was Darnel's old room, which had been barred shut and padlocked years ago. Wolf had no interest in the master bedroom, but Darnel's room, his room was on the other side of that bullet-riddled door.

Every fiber of his being told him to open the door and search for a clue to figure out what had happened to his brother. The respect he held fought this drive ferociously but his need for closure overwhelmed his reverence. Wolf grabbed the doorknob and turned it, only to find the door locked. Taking a step back, Wolf planted his left foot and struck the door with the heel of his right boot. The door frame splintered as the door flew open from the blow.

The room was dark and musky; the curtains had been pulled shut and seemed to be stapled permanently to the wall. The light switch was ripped from its socket and the wires had been cut. "Stay, Beef," Wolf said softly. He entered the room and shut the broken door behind him. Standing in the muggy darkness, Wolf could almost feel the thickness of air permeating throughout the room's atmosphere, adhering itself to his clothes and body. On the desk, there was a pile of newspapers and file folders. Wolf noted that there was no bed in the room, just a mat on the floor in the corner with a wadded blanket and small pillow. A light turned on suddenly from the mat; then just as quickly as it flashed on, it turned back off. Wolf walked slowly across the dimly lit space; the light flashed twice more before he reached it.

He lifted the blanket out of the way and studied the area surrounding the mat a little more closely. The small light flashed again. In the brief flash, Wolf saw a green sleeping bag and a pillow. There was a flashlight wedged in between the wall and the mat; the battery was dying, causing the light to flicker every few seconds. "The only light you can trust is the one you carry," Wolf remembered his brother would always say before a night mission. Wolf laid down on the mat and rested his head on the pillow. He let out a deep, pain-filled sigh, breathing in the scent of the man that used to call this home. Wolf began to cry at the all familiar scent, as he mourned the loss of his brother. Tears flowed down his cheeks once more as he began to sing a sad, old song Johnny Cash had redone years earlier that he and Darnel used to listen to before every mission.

The focus of the song was the pain and sorrow that one may find in life, the pain associated with the discovery that every earthly kingdom is full of ash and rubble. Though it may promise a sound fortress on the outside, destruction and emptiness are always held inside. Wolf and Darnel related to this song as they both had lost friends and loved ones: men and women who had left with a life unfulfilled. Both men viewed this song as a testament to their own life. They believed that when they died, the person that took their life would not receive riches, only realize that they sacrificed much for little to nothing. Therefore, the harder they fought, the less satisfaction their enemy may attain if they were able to defeat them. This gave both Wolf and Darnel confidence and assurance in the face of death.

His voice deep and gravelly, he began to sing their favorite song. He started off soft, remembering that Darnel loved singing the intro. He hummed the next few verses before he hit the main chorus, which he belted out from his lying position. Beef began to howl from the hallway, joining in. Wolf stopped singing, the sobs making it impossible to continue. Beef went silent as his master wept in his brother's refuge.

Finally, Wolf had fallen asleep. He was awoken when he felt something vibrate in his pocket. Wolf reached for it and pulled out Darnel's phone. He forgot he had stuffed it there when he got home. There was an unread message from somebody named Jessica. It read: *Hey, we need you here! Tyrone and his goons are back. Be here as soon as you can. Matt is freaking out!*

Wolf got up from the mat and walked out of the room, trying to make sense of the odd text he read on Darnel's phone. Who was Jessica? Who was Matt? Why was this girl informing him about Tyrone? Had Darnel gotten other people in on his informative work for Detective Westbrooke? Wolf walked into the living room and laid on the couch; Beef made a few attempts to jump up to be with his master and after multiple failures he began to bark. Wolf reached down, grabbing the fat, demanding, little beast. With obvious strain in his muscles, he hoisted him onto the couch next to him. Beef licked his face in gratitude, then put his fat, white butt in the crook of Wolf's arm and laid down once again, resting his head on his master's leg. He was snoring in seconds. Wolf shook his head and slowly started closing his eyes, the questions still flooding his mind as he began to fall asleep.

Memories of his brother, and dangers they had encountered together, flooded into his unconsciousness. Wolf lurched awake instantly, startling Beef awake in the process. After assessing the room and realizing there was no danger, he calmed himself down. He got up from the couch and made his way to the bathroom, Beef hot on his heels. He grabbed four sleeping pills out of the cabinet before walking into the kitchen and downing them with a large glass of water. He went into his room and passed out a half-hour later on his bed, with Beef once again snuggled up next to him.

# Chapter 3

# The Sought Out

June 6th, 2013, 7 a.m. Wolf's home. A pound at the door. "DJ??? DJ, are you home???" Wolf got up groggily, still fully dressed, minus the combat boots. He walked to the door and cracked it open with Beef right at his side.

Wolf looked out the door to see a white man standing on the front stoop; he was wearing jeans and a t-shirt with *NTW* written on the left pectoral. He was a little older than Wolf, probably in his early thirties. The man had a surprised look on his face. *Yes, this is actually my real face,* Wolf thought to himself. It was evident that the man was no cop; his character lacked the common traits and tendencies of law enforcement, though Wolf did sense some leadership in the man. Who was this guy? "Can I help you?" Wolf asked.

"Yes, my name is Matt, Matt Brandt. I'm the pastor of the little white church on the corner of 25th and Welton. I assume you are Will; DJ talks about you all the time," the man answered, extending his hand to Wolf.

Wolf opened the door a little more and took the man's hand, shaking it firmly. "Excuse me Father, but—"

"Pastor," the man interjected.

"Excuse me?" Wolf asked.

"I am a pastor, not a priest. However, I feel more comfortable with being called *Matt,*" the man said with a smile.

Wolf stared at him blankly. "I'm sorry Reverend, Darnel's uh...
he's not here... he's um... he's gone..." Wolf said, trying to choke
back the pain in his voice.

The young pastor had a look of confusion, trying to understand
what Wolf was saying. His face dropped and he lowered his gaze,
staring at the ground for a long hard moment. Then he looked back
into Wolf's eyes, with tears in his own, "I'm very sorry to hear that...
He will definitely be missed on Sunday mornings." Wolf could tell that
the man was genuine. "May I ask when the funeral is so I can pay my
respects?" the pastor continued.

"I uh... I haven't started making the plans yet... There's an
investigation into his death. He was gunned down at about 3 a.m.,
stumbling home from a club yesterday," Wolf responded. The tears
started forming in his eyes as well.

The pastor nodded his head. "That has been happening around
here more and more lately. He was a good man. I hope they catch
whoever did this..." The pastor once again had a look of confusion pass
across his face, "You said DJ was stumbling home from a club?"

Wolf nodded, "That's what he usually did that late at night."

The pastor stared at Wolf for a few more seconds before realization
dawned on his face, "He didn't tell you, did he?"

Wolf lifted his good eyebrow at the pastor, "What exactly didn't
he tell me, Reverend?"

Matt smirked slightly as he realized Wolf was not going to let this
Reverend thing go, "DJ has been going to my church for the past six
months and has been sober for the past five. We have men's Bible study
every Friday night at the church. He would always show up early and
later he would play his guitar and sing until late at night. Actually, he
did that pretty much every night. Always had a case of Red Bull with
him; he'd finish a can every half hour on the dot. Called it his 'miracle
in a can,'" Matt smiled to himself at the memory.

Wolf stood there puzzled at what the pastor had said, "No, that's not possible. I think we're talking about two different people. Darnel hated religion and God—had hated Him for the last twelve years."

"Yes, he had told me about that. But he had asked for forgiveness from God and fell in love with Him. It was quite beautiful, actually." Matt let a single tear roll down his cheek but quickly wiped it away with his hand, "I apologize, I just really grew to respect the man. Can't believe he's gone. At least he's in a better place."

Wolf's body tensed up. *Who is this guy? Who does he think he is saying my brother is in a better place? He's dead! D-E-A-D, dead!* Wolf thought to himself angrily. Keeping his voice calm, he responded to the young pastor standing on his doorstep. "I will have Darnel's funeral planned in a week or so. I will send you an invite." Matt thanked him and then turned to leave.

"You know," Matt said, "It would be an honor to host the service at the church. I'm sure those that he was close to in the congregation would appreciate it."

"Sure, Father," Wolf said; then he shut the door in the pastor's face, locking it right after. His anger boiled as he walked back towards his bedroom.

Wolf Jackson

# Chapter 4

# The Regrets

June 6th, 2013, 10:30 a.m. Beads of sweat dripped from Wolf's head and bare chest as he pounded away at the heavy, synthetic, leather punching bag hanging from a beam in the garage. *How dare he say that I didn't know my own brother?* Wolf thought between his combos on the bag. *Just who does this guy think he is, talking about Darnel like he's known him for years?* Solid thuds sounded throughout the garage with every blow. As the thoughts kept pouring in, Wolf hit the bag harder and harder. Punches began to be followed up by swift kicks and sharp elbows. All his training kicked in as he continued to let out his emotions on the bag.

Changing up his strikes, he ended with a violent spinning heel kick, tearing a large hole into the heavy leather of the bag, as sand poured out onto the ground. Wolf sighed in agitation. He unhooked the bag from the chain and laid it on top of three other freshly torn punching bags. He turned to meet the gaze of the fat white dog laying on a foam pad in the corner. Beef hadn't left his side the past two days. He really lived up to the reputation of a dog being man's best friend.

Wolf sat down on the workout bench and began to dry himself off with the towel that had been hanging off the bar. He then threw the towel to the side and laid down on the bench, grabbing the bar with two 45 pound plates on each side. The overall weight was 225 pounds; he began to do reps of bench press.

*Why would Darnel not tell me about finding God? Sure, I wouldn't have understood, but I would have supported him.* At this point he wasn't even counting anymore; he may have done fifteen reps or so. He racked the bar and sat up. *Was he afraid of me judging him or telling him it was a fool's errand and he knew it?* Wolf dropped to the floor and began to do pushups. *Why did he hide this from me?* Was he ashamed? Wolf stood up from doing maybe fifty pushups or so and looked at his little white companion as he tried to catch his breath.

"What do you think Beef?" he asked. The little white dog just stared at him and tilted his head slightly to the side. "Yeah... I'm in the same boat," Wolf said. He grabbed his towel and slung it around his neck as he walked back into the house through the kitchen, snagging a bottled water and a green apple from the fridge. He bit into the apple as he walked towards his bathroom. He set both on the bathroom counter as he hopped into the shower, turning the water on cold to cool down his body and slow down his rapid heart rate.

All he wanted was for his mind to just relax and go into nothing. It didn't work. After he got done with his shower, he got dressed in his usual attire of khaki cargo pants, black combat boots, and a black hooded sweatshirt. He then went into the kitchen and grabbed his keys from the bowl on the counter. "Let's go for a ride, Beef," he said, as he walked towards the door with his right-hand man on his heels.

He unlocked the door to his truck and bent down to pick up his best friend. With a grunt, he lifted him up and put him in the truck, "You're getting heavy." He chuckled as the dog just *gruffed* in reply. He climbed up into the cab and started the truck, momentarily staring blankly out the windshield, letting the soft guitar riff from the radio fill the silence before putting the truck in gear and driving away.

# Chapter 5

# The Secrets

June 6th, 2013, 11:30 a.m. Wolf drove down the street through the city traffic to 25th and Welton. It wasn't hard to find the church that his brother had hid from him for so many months. It was the only building with a cross outside on the block. The sign reading *Royal Priesthood Church* was a dead give-away as well. Wolf parked just across the street. For some reason, he just couldn't get out of the truck. He knew this feeling all too well. He felt it every time before a firefight. This was the bane of every man. This was fear. He didn't know what he was afraid of; he just knew that he couldn't move.

As he sat there trying to build up the courage to get out of his truck and enter the church, something down the road caught his eye. A red, early '90s, Ford Mustang was parked a little ways down the road with two young kids standing by the driver side. They were leaning down, talking to somebody through the window. The kids couldn't be more than sixteen years old. To the normal person, this wouldn't seem suspicious, but to Wolf, it just didn't seem right. As he watched more closely, he saw the teens pass money through the window. Whoever was in the car handed them two balloons the size of golf balls. They were filled with something. "Drugs," Wolf muttered.

He grabbed his fully loaded Smith and Wesson M&P 45mm from the center consul and opened up his door as he began to exit the truck. "Stay Beef," he said. He tucked the pistol into the back of his pants and tucked the handle underneath his sweatshirt. Wolf took a deep breath and started walking towards the Mustang. The kids stepped away from the car when he was about twenty feet away, and the driver sped off. *He must have seen me and got spooked, but not before I saw his license plate: 529XTM,* Wolf thought to himself. The kids ran away. "Not sure if it's fear of being caught or fear of my face that caused that..." Wolf muttered to himself.

"Hey, Will! Will is that you?" someone shouted from behind him. Wolf turned around to see the pastor that had shown up at his doorstep earlier that morning, walking towards him, waving his hand.

Wolf waved his hand in acknowledgment and walked toward the pastor. "Yeah, how's it going, Reverend?"

"It's Matt, remember?" the young pastor replied. "What brings you down here?"

"I uh, I just wanted to apologize for how I treated you earlier. I'm not in the best of places with what happened to Darnel," Wolf replied.

"Oh, don't worry about that. I didn't take it too personally. People generally respond that way when they are mourning," Matt said. "So why were you down the road? The church is right up there," he said, pointing his thumb over his shoulder.

"I think I just witnessed a drug deal to kids," Wolf said bluntly.

Matt nodded his head, "Probably one of Tyrone's guys. He's a drug lord. He's been selling dope to kids on this block for as long as we've had the church here. We've had more than a few run-ins with him. I can't tell you how many times I have personally called him in for selling drugs to kids, but they never do anything about it. Apparently, they have bigger problems than a man ruining the lives of children," Matt sighed, "But enough about that. Do you want to come inside? We're attempting to plan that funeral for Darnel. A lot of people loved him here."

Wolf gave a shrug of his shoulders and followed the young pastor to the church. As they walked towards the front door, Wolf caught the eye of Beef in the truck. He was standing up on his hind legs, staring at him through the truck window. Wolf made a hand gesture to stay; Beef snorted, then climbed back down into the seat to fall asleep. Wolf just shook his head and continued to follow the young pastor toward the church. He reached the front step leading up to the door and stopped in his tracks. The same fear that had gripped him earlier while he sat in his truck tightened itself around his chest once again.

Something flashed in the corner of his eye; he snapped his head towards it to find himself staring at a bush to the left of him. He felt the grip of his Smith and Wesson M&P in his hand, realizing he was about to pull it, but he stopped himself. "Is everything alright, Will?" the pastor asked him.

Wolf averted his gaze back to the young man who was now standing at the front door, holding it open for him with one hand. "Um, yeah... sorry, Reverend..."

The pastor nodded his head. "It's Matt," he said smiling, "Darnel used to snap into fight mode at times like that too."

"Yeah, kind of comes with the territory of being blown up after witnessing your comrades die," Wolf answered.

Wolf could tell the pastor was unsure how to respond to that one, as he shifted his weight on his feet, still holding the door open for him. "Would you like to come inside?" he asked, smiling at Wolf.

*What is this guy's deal?* Wolf thought to himself. He nodded and walked through the door. "Thanks, Reverend."

The pastor just shook his head, smiling, and let Wolf walk into the small church. It wasn't anything super fancy, just a big open room with wood pews: only two rows of ten. At the end of the room, in front of him, was a small stage with mic stands, a couple guitars, and a drum set. But what really caught Wolf's eye was the picture of his best friend playing his guitar and smiling, being projected onto the white wall above the stage. He looked so happy in that picture, happier than Wolf had seen him in a long time.

"DJ loved playing that guitar of his," the pastor said, noticing the picture himself. There was a young, white woman wearing a gray army t-shirt that was too big for her; she had to tie it in a knot at the bottom behind her to keep it from becoming a dress. She was setting up some candles and flowers around the stage. An attractive red-haired woman was sitting in the front row; she was probably in her early thirties. She was trying to entertain two young boys. "That's my wife and two boys over there," the pastor said, pointing to the woman with the red hair.

Wolf looked over as one of the boys tackled the other and the woman smiled, entertained by their innocence. "Nicely done," he said.

"Thank you," the pastor replied, smiling lovingly towards his family. "As you can see, it's going to take a while to set up, but we will have it ready. We are thinking of having the funeral on the thirtieth. Will that work out for you?"

Wolf took a moment to realize what the pastor had said. When he did, he nodded his head in response. The pastor walked past him to talk to the girl who was still setting stuff up. "Darnel... why wouldn't you have told me how happy this place made you?" Wolf asked silently.

"Will?" the pastor said from the front of the room. "This is Jessica," he said, motioning to the young woman, now facing towards Wolf. "She and DJ were close."

The girl from the text message... Wolf realized.

The woman walked up to him slowly, taken aback by his appearance. After a pause, she held out her hand to shake his. He took it in his own. "It's nice to finally meet you," she said to him with a struggled smile.

Now that she was up close, Wolf could see the redness around her eyes and the smudge of her mascara. She had been crying. But even with the puffy cheeks, giant t-shirt, filthy jeans, and brown hair pulled back in an unkempt bun, she was easily one of the most beautiful women Wolf had ever laid his eyes upon. She was a tiny little thing, no more than five foot and two inches. She *maybe* weighed a hundred and twenty pounds, but that seemed doubtful. Even with the oversized shirt, he could tell she was athletic. She appeared to be in her early twenties.

"It's nice to meet you too," Wolf said, stumbling over his words as he stared into her magnificent blue eyes. "What do you mean by *finally meet me?*"

"Oh, DJ used to talk about you all the time. He really admired you," she said with that stunning smile. Wolf couldn't help but smile very briefly back at her before the pain hit, remembering his brother. Her smile faded as well, into a look of compassion. "I am so, so sorry for your loss," she said, then tears started flowing hot down her cheeks. "I'm sorry. Excuse me," she barely choked out, before she turned and walked over to a doorway at the left side of the room, disappearing into the hallway beyond it.

"She's taking DJ's death pretty hard," the pastor said, as Wolf stared after her. "Like I said, they were close. She helped him through a lot, and well, he seemed to be an answer to her prayers…"

Wolf looked at him, raising his one eyebrow, "What do you mean, Rabbi?"

Matt shook his head, "Jessica's older brother, Jason, died due to a heroin overdose last year. He was only twenty-four years old. He had come back from the army and was just broken. Tyrone was the one that sold the dope to him. The cops haven't done anything, no matter how many times we call to report him dealing drugs to kids. She was praying for some justice and then DJ showed up one Friday night. He was drunk and stumbling down the street, trying to find his way home. He saw Tyrone dealing drugs to some teenagers and he intervened."

Matt smiled at the memory. "Jess and I were outside, both heading to our cars when we heard the yelling. DJ was calling Tyrone a low-life. He used much more colorful language than that of course. Tyrone went to put hands on him and then he was on the ground. I had never seen a man get hit so fast in my life. I didn't even see the blow, just DJ shaking the pain out of his hand afterward.

"Tyrone didn't know how to react. He ran off and then DJ told the kids to go home. I drove him to his house that night and asked him to call me in the morning. He did and I asked him if he wanted to have coffee with me. He said yes and we went to Jess' mom's coffee shop. She was so happy to see him, she kept trying to give him a whole bunch of stuff for free," he chuckled, shaking his head remembering that, "She wouldn't take no for an answer, even when he said he doesn't do church. She told him just to try it; she's pretty spunky when she wants to be. He agreed to try it and, from then on, he showed up every single Friday night and Sunday morning. I personally think it was originally for Jess," he said smiling, "but he stayed for Jesus."

Wolf sat taking all of this in. His brother had a whole secret life that he didn't share with him. All he could do is wonder, *Why? Why would he hide this? Why wouldn't he tell his best friend any of this?* "I sense that you're a little upset by all this. Are the pictures too much for you right now?" Matt asked, a look of genuine concern on his face.

Wolf met his gaze, realizing tears were starting to form in his eyes once more. He cleared his throat real quick, "No, Reverend… I uh, I just didn't know about any of this…"

Matt went to say something but hesitated. "It must be hard having him hide something like this from you. He told me how close you guys were. Once again, I am terribly sorry for your loss, Will."

Wolf nodded. "I'm uh, I'm going to head out. Thank you for inviting me inside, Rabbi. Shalom," Wolf said, as he turned and headed for the door he had used to enter the small sanctuary.

Matt smiled and shook his head, "Come back anytime, God bless."

The door shut behind Wolf as he entered the Denver heat. He crossed the street and opened up the door to his truck, revealing his fat companion snoozing on his seat. "Get to your side, Beef." The dog lazily opened his eyes, saw his master, and slowly dragged himself to the passenger side where he instantly fell back asleep. Wolf climbed into his seat and started up the truck; the radio turned on and the speakers came to life yet again. He placed the big truck into drive, joining the heavy Denver traffic, allowing the music to carry his thoughts away as distant memories.

Wolf Jackson

# Chapter 6

# The Hurts

June 6th, 2013, 3:00 p.m. Wolf sat on his brother's mat, once again unwilling to move. The last thirty-six hours felt like an eternity. There was so much pain and confusion, Wolf didn't know how to cope. He began to sing that same sad song once more, in a hope to keep his brother close, but his sadness deepened as his stronghold felt more like a prison. The futile battle cry echoed in hollowed out walls. That cry died long before Darnel did; Wolf had just been clinging to a ghost, and no ghost was worth dying for.

After much sobbing, Wolf left the mat and went to wash his face. He leaned on his bathroom counter, staring blankly at the mirror in front of him. Then he quickly averted his gaze to the sink, realizing there was a mirror in front of him. He breathed deeply and slowly looked up again. Now he was staring at himself, face to face for the first time in two years. He sure looked like a monster. Why wouldn't someone hide from him? He turned his gaze and walked away from the mirror, trying to forget his own personal scars, both physical and emotional.

The doorbell rang and Beef started barking. "Now what?" Wolf muttered under his breath as he walked out of his room to answer the front door. When he opened it, he was once again graced by the most beautiful woman he had ever seen... Jessica.

This time she was wearing a black blouse and much nicer jeans than before. She had her beautiful, brown hair down. She had redone her mascara, but he had seen her earlier with it smudged all over her face. Even then, she didn't need it. She smiled at him, this time not even fazed by his appearance.

"Hi, Will. Or do you prefer Wolf? I know DJ used to call you that and…" she trailed off as a slight tremor threatened to break her radiant smile, but she quickly corrected herself. "I'm not intruding, am I?" she asked, blinking those big blue eyes of hers.

He stared at her for a moment longer, trying to catch his breath. *Wow, this woman is gorgeous…* he thought. He noticed her smile had faded as she stared at him quizzically. *Say something! Come on man!*

"Hi, uh no, you're uh, you're not intruding, and you can call me either," he finally squeezed out.

She smiled again and instantly stole his breath away once more. "Do you mind if I come in?" she asked awkwardly, as she shifted from one foot to the other.

He stared at her blankly again for a moment. "Yeah, sure," he said, as he opened the door more and stepped to the side so she could walk in. He caught himself staring at her legs as she passed. He could see the muscles in her calves through the material of her jeans: not huge, but defined. Beef came running right up to her, snorting and wagging his little tail. She bent down to pet him and Wolf quickly averted his gaze from her.

"What a cute doggie!" she said as she scratched his head, cooing at him. "What's his name?" she asked, now looking up at Wolf.

He was once again met by her gaze and was entranced by those eyes. "Beef," he said.

"Awww, that's adorable!" she said, as she continued to pet and scratch him all over. The fat little beast was loving the attention for sure.

"So um, how can I help you?" Wolf asked.

"Oh yeah, sorry," she said, smiling as she gave Beef one last pat and stood up. "I just wanted to see how you're holding up. Matt said you left pretty abruptly."

"Oh, I'm uh, I've been better… I just lost my best friend so I'm pretty messed up, and on top of that, he had a whole secret life that he was too afraid to tell me about," Wolf responded. *Woah. How did she just make me admit that?* he thought to himself.

She looked at him with compassionate eyes, "DJ wanted to tell you everything, he just wasn't sure how. He was trying to make sense of it all himself."

Wolf nodded, "Yeah, that's understandable… so were you two together or something?" he asked.

She laughed at that one. "No. I wanted to be at first, but he didn't seem interested and truly I loved him more like a brother than anything else," she said, as her eyes started to water up slightly.

Wolf moved to comfort her, out of sheer instinct, when luckily the doorbell rang once more. "I gotta get that real quick," he said, as he walked over to the door. *Get a handle on yourself, Wolf.*

Wolf opened up the door to reveal the blonde-haired detective standing on his doorstep. "How can I help you, Ma'am?"

She sort of smiled, though it was strained. "I prefer Detective; my navy days are behind me," she said. "How are you holding up?"

"I'm fine," he responded. "What can I do for you?"

"Can we talk in private? I wasn't able to explain the details of the case to you at the station." Her words were hesitant yet thought out.

Wolf looked apologetically at Jess and stepped out the door, shutting it behind him so that he and the detective were alone on the porch. Wolf looked at the blonde woman quizzically, "What haven't you told me?"

She took a deep breath and handed him a file folder. It was light, maybe ten pages in it. "I nabbed this from my captain's desk; it was full of documents when he took it from me. There is not much in there, but hopefully it will help."

Wolf opened the folder to reveal some pictures of a large house surrounded by trees and a high brick wall with a wrought iron gate. There was another of a man smoking a cigar, wearing a dress shirt and vest with a tie; he was talking to a younger guy dressed in a baggy shirt and a flat bill cap. There were a few pictures of vehicles: a blue Chevy Camaro, a black Hummer, and a couple Cadillac Escalades. The last picture was of a red Ford Mustang; Wolf recognized it as the one outside the church the day before. Sticky notes were attached to the pictures with time and date stamps written in pen: Darnel's handwriting. Behind them was a stack of notes, written on notebook paper. These notes consisted of route schedule and the coming and going of vehicles.

Wolf looked up from his folder and raised his one eyebrow at the detective, "Why are you giving this to me?"

She shifted her weight from one foot to the other and back. Her body posture told him that she was going to say something that he did not want to hear. "We uh…. We've decided to close his case… His body will be released for burial in the next few days."

Wolf stared at her blankly. Anger began to build inside him like a churning volcano. "What do you mean you are closing his case? He was your informant! What happened to a week?" Wolf exclaimed angrily. He heard the door open behind him, but he was in too much of a rage to turn around and see what was going on.

Something soft and warm grabbed his arm and he looked back to see Jessica holding onto him. He locked his eyes on her hand for a moment as she held onto his bare arm. He didn't like it when people touched him, especially if he was already upset, but her touch…. her touch soothed him instantly. He looked at her face to realize that her eyes were directly locked on his. Her eyes were soft yet stern. He knew what she was saying, just by staring into those eyes: *Let me take care of this,* they said. Wolf nodded his head and stepped back so that she could address the other woman. Her hand left his arm with a gentle touch, leaving Wolf with butterflies in his stomach.

He couldn't take his eyes off her as she approached the detective. "Hi, my name is Jessica and I was a close friend of Darnel's. Why aren't you furthering his case?"

The detective shook her hand, "Nice to meet you. I am so very sorry for your loss. As for your friend's case… there just isn't any substantial evidence to support the pretense of a pre-meditated murder. As much as I want to continue to pursue it, my captain has decided to shut it down. It is out of my control. I am so sorry.

"There were no witnesses, no shell casings, and the bullet was destroyed on impact. Even if all that didn't come into play, there are so many black-market guns in this city that aren't registered. We would never find the murder weapon. We have nothing."

Jessica stood there for a moment, staring at the other woman in front of her. Wolf could only stare at her in amazement; she was keeping her emotions in check so well. "What about traffic cameras, tread marks, or maybe somebody got a glimpse of the car?"

The detective shifted her feet once more, "We couldn't get a warrant for the cameras and nobody saw anything. There's nothing we can do. That's why I gave Will the file."

Jessica nodded her head, anger now prominent on her face, but she still managed to keep her tone in check, "Our judicial system is so twisted that your department won't even attempt to dig deeper to find the murderer of a man that served our country and became a highly decorated marine and served with honor? Even though your entire department and I both know who is responsible for his death and at least forty others in the past three years?"

The detective took a deep breath and looked right at Jessica, "Since you were friends with Darnel, did he ever tell you about his friend Kate?" she asked.

Jess's eyes widened. "You're Kate?" she asked.

The detective nodded and tears began to form in her eyes, "I don't know how much he told you, but believe me, he meant just as much to me as he did to you." She paused and looked at Wolf, "Well, maybe not as much as you. He told me how close you were."

Wolf's eyes widened, "Detective, I think you have some things you need to tell me."

The detective nodded, "Darnel was more than just my informant. I knew his wife, Delilah," she said.

Will's jaw felt like it was going to hit the floor: Delilah, the wife Darnel had lost but never wanted to talk about. He had been waiting for Darnel to tell him about her for years but he would never open up. Wolf didn't even know how he lost her, just that it destroyed him inside.

"How did you know Delilah?" Wolf asked.

"She and I grew up together; we were really close through middle school and high school. We met up a few times when they moved back to Denver after her parents gave them the house as a wedding present. It's how I knew your address," the detective said.

Wolf did not know what to say to her. After a long moment he asked the one question he never got Darnel to answer, "What happened to her?" he asked.

Kate sighed and looked at the ground. "I am not entirely sure what happened or how it happened. I just know there was a car accident. Honestly, I don't even know who was driving or if they were both in the car. I just know she didn't make it."

Jess looked at the ground, "I didn't know what happened either. Darnel just said you were a friend of hers. How are you holding up?" she asked.

The detective wiped tears from her eyes and nodded her head, "I will be okay, just feel like I am losing her all over again. Darnel was a good man. He helped a lot of people."

Wolf took a deep breath and let it out slowly. Jess nodded her head and smiled through her tears, "He really was, but he is so much better now. He finally got to see Delilah again."

Wolf didn't know exactly what Jessica meant, but he could tell she found solace in it. His own mind was twisting and shattering his resolve at every turn, and he began to tremble. The floor felt like it was about ready to drop out from underneath his boots. He began to hear faint gunfire and mortar strikes; the walls replaced with brick buildings and sand.

Anxiety and fear threatened to blow a chasm into his chest, leaving only the void in the place of bone and flesh. Just when he felt the chasm would take over, swallowing him into its depths, he felt a soft hand once again on his bicep. The bricks and sand faded into cool Denver air and the familiarity of his front porch. He looked over and saw Jessica once again holding onto his arm and staring into his eyes. She rubbed his arm lovingly and smiled. "You alright Will?" she asked.

He nodded his head, "Just need some more rest, I guess."

Jessica rubbed his arm some more and nodded her head before removing her hand from his arm. She turned back to the detective, "Kate, I think we should let Will get some rest, but I would love to go get coffee with you if you would like."

Kate smiled and nodded, "I would very much like that, thank you."

Jessica patted Wolf's arm again, "When you feel up to it, we could go get coffee too. I want to get to know the man that Darnel respected so much." Wolf looked at her and nodded. Jessica smiled, "Okay, you let me know." And with that, both women walked off the porch to their cars, and drove off, leaving Wolf standing alone.

# Chapter 7

# The Judged

June 7th, 2013, 9:00 p.m. Wolf sat on his bed, staring at his wall. The papers from the file the detective had given him were now pinned to the wall with red, green, and blue strings connecting them all together in certain ways. Blue stood for the relationships between the pictures of individuals leading to the cars, the buildings, and other people to discern the hierarchy. The green stood for the timestamps of when certain people and certain vehicles were at certain places. The red stood for the distribution patterns connecting the people to locations: some had two lines of string, others were single, showing if the quantity was distributed twice a week or more. At the very top of the web was a picture of the man in the expensive suit, the man that took Darnel's life: Tyrone, or *Aspect*, as his men called him.

His heart was thumping in his ears. He inhaled deeply in his nostrils and exhaled slowly through his mouth. The information that the detective had given to him earlier that day flooded through his mind. This Tyrone character was a real tool. He had been selling drugs to kids for the past three years. His organization had caused the deaths of dozens due to overdose and other instances believed to be more violent. People had tried to stand up to him in the past: they wound up missing or beaten. There had been those who tried to get a lawsuit against him; all the evidence was either disproven or not substantial enough.

This guy was smart. He knew the law and how it worked, which also made it so he knew how to avoid being caught: whether it was paying off the right official, killing the right witness, or putting the blame on somebody in the wrong place at the wrong time. The only way to stop him would be a hand-written confession followed by a sworn statement. Either that or incriminating video evidence catching him in the act. Wolf had run into these types of men before overseas, both in Syria and Afghanistan. Most of them were arms dealers and terrorists. All of them were the same: a cancer to everyone and everything around them. If there was anything he learned from his time overseas, it was that cancers had to be cut out from the roots. Their entire organization had to be wiped out, gathering all the evidence possible through wire-tapping, video recordings, pictures, and psychological warfare.

He got up and walked over to his wardrobe, opening it to reveal a cache of weapons. To the right was a Remington 700 .308 sniper rifle with a shoulder strap, gunmetal black, custom-built thermal scope that converted to a red-dot, foldable bipod, and tactical suppressor. Next to that, sat a customized M4 assault rifle with a foregrip, twelve extended magazines, M68 Close Combat Optic sight, with tactical suppressor. To the left of that was a Remington Tactical pump action 12 gage with five extended magazines and a box of buckshot right next to it.

Hanging from the door was two pistols, both Smith & Wesson M&P .45 ACP's. One was full size, the other was a shield compact, both Mod 2 matte black with night sights and detachable suppressors. The full size was in a holster that concealed inside the waistband on the small of the back in the door cubby. The shield was also in the cubby attached to the door, stored in its hard-shell holster that was meant to slide into a large pocket safely. Ten magazines sat on the shelf directly below it, five double stacks for the full size and five single stacks for the shield, all fully loaded with tactical hollow points. Under that was a combat knife in a boot sheath.

A black leather street biker's jacket hung from the other door, with a built-in black hood from a hooded sweatshirt. A plain white t-shirt was on the hangar inside of it. Wolf took off his sweatshirt and tank-top, keeping his dark brown cargo pants and combat boots on. He grabbed the jacket off the door and laid it on the bed. He took off his dog tags, kissed them, and tucked them in his pocket.

Turning back to the bed, he put on the white t-shirt. He then put the full-size M&P with his holster in the back of his pants, sliding the t-shirt over the handle. He grabbed the double stack magazines and tucked them into the hidden sleeves inside the tactical pockets on the left leg of his pants. Then, he put on the leather jacket; he grabbed the shield and slid it with the holster into the inside left breast pocket. He then took the single stack magazines and placed them in the custom pockets he had on the right breast pocket that were just big enough to hold the magazines. Then, he strapped the combat knife inside his right boot.

Inside the right, front jacket pocket, were tactical gloves; he pulled them out and slide them on. In the left, front jacket pocket was a black tactical mask that covered basically the entire face and head, except the eyes and bridge of the nose. Wolf stared at it long and hard and then put it back into the pocket of his jacket. Reaching into the wardrobe one more time he grabbed the Remington 700 .308 and slung it over his right shoulder. He grabbed the three extra mags and stuffed them into his pocket on the right leg of his cargo pants. He then grabbed the M4 and put the sling around his neck, sliding the magazines into his rear pockets.

On the dresser sat another pair of dog tags. Wolf picked them up and read the name *Lieutenant Darnel Jones* inscribed within the metal. Dried blood flawed parts of the shiny chrome: Darnel's blood. He put the chain around his neck and the tags dangled at his chest. Then, he dawned the mask and looked into the mirror, staring the figure before him directly in the eyes. There was a cancer that infected this city. It had to be removed. Tonight, he would be the scalpel.

Without a word, he walked out of the bedroom and into the kitchen where he grabbed a green apple. He stuffed it into his pocket as he walked towards the garage. "Stay Beef," he muttered, as he walked through the door and closed it behind him. He walked past his lifting equipment, to the far wall of the garage, reached up to the top of the door jamb, and grabbed the key that had been resting there. He unlocked the door.

He walked into the other half of his garage and switched on the light. A soft buzz resounded through the dark space as the area lit up to reveal a covered vehicle. He pulled off the cover slowly, with one hand, to reveal a true American classic. Wolf stood before a sleek, glossy, marble black, 1969, custom manual, 4-speed, Chevy Chevelle SS, with dark tinted windows, 18-inch sport tires, and 369s V8 big block. Wolf slid his hand across the hood, noting the perfect placing of the glossy white dual pinstripes. This was a classic beauty of a machine; he couldn't help but admire her as he walked over to the driver side.

This was Darnel's prized possession, his one true love, his baby. He had built this car from the ground up, all on his own, complete with custom interior and custom paint job. It was all done by Darnel. She was pristine, not a single scratch blemished her body. Wolf had only gotten to ride in it a few times on road trips with Darnel before the PTSD had taken him too far into himself and drove him to alcoholism. He would, however, take her out for a ride once a week and then wash her down, polishing her once a month. Wolf opened the already unlocked driver side door and slid the rifles onto the back seat, placing the magazines into the ammunition box that sat on the floorboard behind the driver seat.

He sat down on the black, leather bench seat, behind the wheel. Reaching up to the visor, he flipped it down, letting the keys fall into his hand. Pressing the button on the passenger side visor, he watched as the garage door opened. Putting in the clutch, he turned the key in the ignition. She roared to life. A smile swelled up under his mask. "Still the prettiest girl in Denver," he said, as he rested his hand on the dashboard lightly. He pushed *play* on the cassette player and the speakers sputtered to life and filled the car with his brother's music.

Wolf drove out of his garage and pulled away from the driveway, rumbling down the road and into the night. Jessica had told him that Tyrone lived in a huge, white house with black trim, on the corner of 29th and Avery, only two blocks from the church. Wolf found it easily. He drove by it and circled around the block. He parked down on a side street, around the corner from the house, in the darkest part of the street he could find. This way, he could be somewhat concealed. Tyrone's house was on a hill about seventy yards from the main road. He had a large, grassy yard with a long, winding driveway, entrenched by large planter boxes with trimmed hedges. The yard was surrounded by a high, stone wall and a large gate. There were two men stationed by the gate, not really paying attention to the road. There was also a camera pointed towards the road that Wolf took note of. This was going to be harder than originally thought.

Leaving the rifles in the car, he traveled on foot, down the street, towards the house. He stuck to the shadows, silent and swift, as he was taught in the service. He moved more like a phantom than a man, there one second and gone in the next. Every step was calculated and perfectly executed. Wolf was now concealed in the shadows, across the street from the corner portion of the high brick wall. There was a medium-sized tree a few feet away from the wall. Wolf smiled under his mask, now seeing his way in. He made sure there were no cars coming then bolted across the street. He ran up the base of the trunk and pushed off with one foot, grasping the top of the wall with his hands, then pulling himself up and over. Landing silently onto the well-trimmed lawn, he then turned to face the main property.

He watched in silence, observing the layout of the yard, mapping a route to the front door. There were five vehicles parked in the driveway: a Honda Civic, a large Chevy Silverado, a lifted Jeep Wrangler, a new Dodge Charger, and the red Mustang he had seen earlier that day. There were two men on the front porch, both were smoking and too busy talking to one another. Wolf observed that the man on the left was around 5'10, 185 pounds; the man on the right was around 6'4, 230 pounds. Both were capable of handling themselves in a fight and were packing. One had a Glock tucked down the front of his shirt. The other had a .44 magnum revolver sitting next to him on the guard rail of the porch. Who knew how many men were inside?

Wolf crept closer until he was just outside the revealing glare of the porch light. He drew his M&P full-size and screwed a suppressor onto the barrel. There was an exterior light over the heads of the men. Taking aim with his pistol, Wolf shot the light bulb. The porch went dark. The two men froze briefly in shock, and for a moment, their guard was down. Wolf made his move; holstering his pistol, he sprinted across the grass, vaulted the handrail and engaged the porch smokers. He could see the man with the Glock reaching for his weapon, still oblivious to the new third party. He never saw Wolf coming. With a swift, left hook, Wolf dropped him to the hard, wood planks on the porch.

The taller man reached for his revolver on the handrail next to him. Before he could reach it, a hand gripped his wrist like a vise, followed by a sharp elbow to his temple. Dazed, the man lay on the floor of the porch; he began to lift himself off the ground when a hard boot faded his world into black. Wolf pulled the laces out of the men's boots and used them to bind the two men together. He took both of their phones and slipped a bug into each before placing them back into their pockets. Then, he took a note out of his pocket that simply said, *For the sake of Justice.* He grabbed a knife from one of the fallen men and used it to drive the note into the solid oak door.

Wolf heard a commotion coming from the other side of the door. The door handle began to turn. Diving off the porch, Wolf ducked behind the Charger as the light from the inside of the house flooded onto the porch from the open door. He heard yelling coming from the porch and footsteps heading towards the vehicle. On his knee, Wolf drew his pistol, firing two rounds at a dark figure that had appeared at the front of the car. The figure collapsed onto the Jeep behind it, setting off the alarm. The figure crashed to the ground. Wolf ran to him and found the man unconscious. He felt for a pulse; it was weak. With the alarm still blaring, Wolf needed to make his move. Rounding the front end of the Mustang, he bolted to the side of the house. He heard the commotion of men running to aid their fallen companion, followed by somebody shouting for someone to get the keys to one of the cars. Then a voice more authoritative than the others silenced the rest.

Wolf peaked around the corner, seeing a man in a suit with his back to him: Tyrone. "Get him to the ER. Strip all his weapons off him, his shoes, phone, and his ID. Leave no connection to any of us. You know the drill; drop him off in front of the ER, say nothing to no one, drive off. Take the Suburban from the garage and change the plates before you get back. Go!"

Men jumped into action with one running to the garage to retrieve the vehicle. Two more carried the wounded man after him. "Now the rest of you," Tyrone said to the remaining twelve or so, "find the intruders; comb the property. Now!" Wolf looked over and saw a dumpster up against the brick wall, about sixty yards away. It was now or never: he ran in a dead sprint to the dumpster, jumped up it, and vaulted over the wall. There were some shouts. A couple shots were fired while he was running, but he had already disappeared into the shadows once more. Returning to the Chevelle, he started her up and got out of the area before anyone could even see his car, taking every alley and back way he could to get home, to make sure no one followed him.

# Chapter 8

# The Shadows

Wolf stood in a dark alley. Everything seemed off-kilter as if the world was on a boat being rocked back and forth by the ocean. A man lay on the ground bleeding from his chest, ribcage, and abdomen. A knife dangled loosely from Wolf's hand, thick scarlet liquid dripping from the cold steel glowing in the moonlight. A hand gripped his shoulder, whipping him around. Darnel stood before him, clenching Wolf's arm like a vise. He took the knife from Wolf's hand and wiped down the blade and handle, using a white towel, and dropped them both to the ground. He was screaming something at Wolf, gripping both of his shoulders now. His voice sounded garbled like Wolf was under water, rapidly becoming more and more audible as if he was nearing the surface. "We have to go!" Darnel shouted at him and dragged Wolf out of the alley.

June 8th, 2013, 9 a.m. Wolf awoke, jerking upright in his bed, pistol at the ready. His heart pounded in his chest as his brain tried to assess the situation. The dark alley had vanished; he was now in his room with Beef at his side. He was shirtless and wearing loose-fitting pajama pants. His rifle, knife, and jacket were once again hidden in his wardrobe. The Chevelle was parked in her hideaway again. Wolf's stomach churned as he began to recall the night before. He rushed into his bathroom and blew chunks into the toilet. He had killed again...

The emotions poured out of him like a raging waterfall. He wept and emptied the contents of his stomach until he was dry heaving. He lay on the cold tile of the bathroom floor. He had no strength in his body to move. His blood ran cold through his body, causing him to shake violently. Sweat began to pour down his face, chest, and back. He lay there for what seemed to be an eternity, as he drifted in and out of consciousness, before he finally blacked out.

June 8th, 2013, 10:30 a.m. Soft hands caressed his face. A velvety, urgent voice filled his head, "Will!... Will! Will, wake up please!" His eyes fluttered open slightly. "That's it, Will! That's it! Wake up!" His eyes began to open more and more. His eyes opened dully to reveal Jessica staring down at him, worry eminent on her face. "Are you okay, Will?"

"Jessica?" Wolf managed to say in a hoarse voice. "How did you get in here?" he asked. His throat felt like it had been torn up on the inside.

"I knocked on your door for half an hour and you didn't respond. I was worried, so I used the key Darnel gave me and opened the door. I found you lying on the floor with vomit in the toilet," she said. Before he could respond, she shoved a bottle of water in his face. "You need to drink this," she said sternly.

He nodded and sat up, leaning his back against the wall, and began to drink the water. Jessica was leaning against the cabinets below the sink, across from him. She stared at him with those amazing eyes, seeming to be satisfied that he was actually drinking something. After he had finished a little less than half the bottle, she asked if he was feeling better; Wolf nodded. "Good," she said, "Clean yourself up; you're covered in sweat. I will be in the living room." She then got up and walked out of the bathroom, closing the door behind her. "Drink that water!" she hollered through the closed door.

"Yes ma'am," Wolf responded, and drank from the bottle once more, before setting it on the counter. With some effort, he pulled himself to his feet and stepped into the hot shower to clean himself up. After the shower, he went into his room, putting on his usual attire of tan cargo pants, a black sweatshirt, and combat boots. Walking into the living room, he found Jessica sitting on the couch with Beef cuddled up to her hip. She noticed him entering the room and smiled that breathtaking smile. "Glad to see you back on your feet," she said.

He couldn't help but smile back at her, "I guess I have you to thank for that."

She continued to smile at him for a few moments and then stood up. "Well, comes with the job. I am a nurse at Independence Hospital, just a few miles away," she replied.

Wolf raised his good eyebrow, "I didn't know you were a nurse."

"Yeah, well, I guess you've got a lot to learn about me," she said, then winked. "And from what I gather, I have a lot to learn about you as well."

Wolf cocked his head, "I'm not quite sure what you're getting at."

She pursed her lips, trying to figure out how to phrase what she was going to say next. "One of Tyrone's goons showed up last night with two bullet holes in his chest. They dropped him right in front of the ER and bailed, but I have seen him around before and know he works for Tyrone. He made it; would only say a masked figure shot him when he was out for a stroll."

Wolf held her gaze; her eyes were intense. He remained silent as she stared at him for a few moments. "Is this a statement or an accusation?" he asked.

She ran her tongue against the inside of her bottom lip. "What did you do, Will?" she asked.

Wolf thought about lying to her. He had already made up a lie last night to tell the police, while he was hiding his weapons. But as his mouth attempted to tell her said lie, he instead let out a long sigh and looked at the ground. After a second, he allowed himself to make eye contact. "He killed Darnel." Tears started to form in his eyes but he kept eye contact with her. "I defend my country; it's what I was trained to do. I faced monsters like this guy overseas. They take whatever they want, with money, and if that doesn't work, they take it through the barrel of a gun. This sort of animal is a stigma that won't go away on its own. They must be dug out at the root, extracting their whole organization. The Marines trained me to be a scalpel that removes these stigmas. It's what I know..."

She stared at him, tears forming in her own eyes. "He owns the judicial system, Will. You heard them; they aren't going to do anything!" tears flowed hot down her cheeks. "I don't want to lose you too. You are all I have left of DJ, and I won't let you kill yourself by enacting vengeance!"

Wolf chuckled slightly, "You sound like Darnel." A brief flash of the alleyway from his dream went through his mind, but he dismissed it as soon as it appeared. "What I am going after is evidence. Vengeance is not the goal, justice is. All I want is justice."

Jess looked at him, "What about the man in the ER last night? He almost died, Will."

Wolf nodded, "That was a mistake. I went in reckless and got sloppy. Reckless and sloppy acts always lead to death... I can't afford any more death..."

"William Jackson, you listen to me," Jessica said, "You cannot lose yourself to this. If you are going to do this, you must do it right. No more going in half-cocked, neurotic and emotional. If you can't, then don't. Promise me that no matter what happens, you will stay true to who you are and hold firm to your core values, no matter what." He nodded his head. "Alright then," she said, as she wiped the tears from her eyes.

She sat back down on the couch next to Beef. The little white dog lifted his head, wagged his tail, and snorted at her as she started to give him attention again. Wolf sat in a chair, directly across from her. He leaned forward with his elbows on his knees and stared at her. After a moment or so, she caught him staring, and met his gaze. She raised her eyebrow quizzically at him.

He cleared his throat and wiped tears from his eyes and then met her gaze once again. "You realize if I continue to take out Tyrone's whole organization... I will have to hurt people. I'll have to become the darkness inside me."

She nodded her head and then leaned forward with her elbows on her knees just like him. She stared right into his eyes. "Will, everyone has their own personal darkness inside of them. But there is a light that no darkness can withstand, not even yours. You don't have to go dark, you just have to find that light."

Wolf gritted his teeth. "There's something you need to know about me," he said. She just cocked an eyebrow at him. "When I got back from Afghanistan, I got low, real low. I got involved with drugs and alcohol. First it was only pain killers and maybe a few beers a night, but then it got worse. I got into heroin, and when I didn't have heroin, I had whiskey. I lost everything. My job as security at a bank, my house, my car, my fiancé, even Beef... my injuries made me angry and I didn't know how to live with this face..." His hand shook as he reached up to touch the marred flesh. "My fiancé wouldn't even kiss me. Who could blame her? How could anyone love the monster that I had become?"

A tear trickled down Jess's face, but she stayed silent as he continued to tell his story. "Somewhere along the line, somebody told Darnel what was going on with me, so he came looking for me. He found me late one night in a dark alley with a knife in my hand and a dead man at my feet. I had gotten in a drunken brawl with the guy in a bar. The bartender told us to take it outside, so we did. Even in my drunken state, the man couldn't touch me. I was winning the fight and he knew it, so he pulled a knife…" His voice trailed off as he remembered grabbing the guy's knife hand as the man tried to stab him, twisting it violently and driving the blade deep into the man's chest, ribcage, and stomach. He watched, yet again, as the man crashed to the ground, his blood spilling onto the pavement. He cleared his throat, realizing that he had stopped talking. "Darnel grabbed me and cleaned up the evidence. He put me in his car and began yelling at me."

Yet again his mind pictured the memory of driving down the road, riding in the passenger seat, Darnel screaming at him, "This isn't Afghanistan, Wolf! You can't kill a man in an alleyway in a drunken brawl and get away with it! Promise me right now that you will never take another life unless you absolutely have to! Promise me!" Wolf nodded his head, staring at the man's blood on his hands. "Now you and I are going to have each other's back, just like in Afghanistan. I'm going to take you to my place and we're going to get you cleaned up. I've got you, my brother."

"He took me here to his house and cleaned me up. I didn't know it, but Darnel went back into the bar and said a man got mugged in the alley and he chased him off. The man survived because of Darnel. He was the only family I had left… I had gotten in a few drunken brawls after that night, but he intervened. He was the reason that I kept those demons deep inside… now that he's gone… they've been released…"

"I don't believe that," Jess said bluntly.

Wolf raised his good eyebrow at her, "What part?"

"That Darnel was the only reason that you kept your demons deep down."

"Why do you say that?" he asked.

She leaned closer to him so she could look even deeper into his eyes, "Because I've seen the heart of the man that battles those demons. And it's beautiful. You might be embracing the darkness that is inside of you, but the man that's inside of you will take control over his demons once again."

"How can you be so sure of that?" he asked her.

"Like I said before, Will: I've seen your heart, and it's beautiful," she said. "You are a good man, Will, and what you're doing does not make you a bad person. Your actions don't define who you are, they only refine you. Have you ever heard about David from the Bible?"

Wolf was about to object to her throwing scripture at him, but he was intrigued. "No, I have not."

"David was the king of Jerusalem long ago; he was a man of God. Yet he killed tens of thousands of men. He was a warrior; he fought for his people, his country. He killed his first man when he was a teenager. The man he killed was a giant named Goliath that had challenged the Israelite army to have one on one combat with him to decide the victor of the battle. He was so huge and ferocious that all the men were afraid to fight him. The king at the time, Saul, sent out for somebody to fight the giant. Nobody would do it. David went out to bring food to the frontlines for his older brothers and he saw the giant boasting about his strength on the frontline of the enemy army. David saw how terrified his countrymen were and he went to the king and told him that he would kill the giant.

"Now, Saul was nervous about sending a boy to kill a giant monster of a man. David wouldn't back down. David knew that this giant had to die in order to save the lives of innocent women and children. After much prayer, he challenged the giant with a sling and a stone. As the giant laughed, mocking him, David loaded his sling and launched the stone, catching the giant in the head, and dropped him to the ground where David then decapitated him with his own sword. His actions saved the lives of an entire civilization. And for years to come, he was in battle after battle, fighting for his life and the life of his people.

"He was a warrior, Will, just like you. He didn't kill for pleasure; he killed to save the lives of the innocent. However, there was one man that he had murdered: Uriah. David had slept with Uriah's wife, Bathsheba, while Uriah was at war. She got pregnant and David tried to trick Uriah into sleeping with his wife, so he would think that the child was his. But Uriah was too worried about the men he left in the battle and would not leave David's presence. David sent him back with his own death warrant: orders for Uriah to be placed in the most vulnerable position on the frontlines, and the men to fall back at the last moment, allowing him to be taken. Uriah was so loyal, he did not read the note that he had carried back to the army, and he suffered for it. David thought he had gotten away with it, taking Bathsheba as his bride, but the prophet Nathan called him out and the child died shortly after childbirth a year later. David wept and repented with a broken and contrite heart before the Lord. Do you know what happened then?"

Wolf shook his head and shrugged. "God glorified David as a man after His own heart," she said. "You see, the Lord didn't look at the beast inside the man—the adulterous, murderous thief, but the heart that had been manipulated by it. Will, you're a modern-day David, you just don't know it yet." Wolf raised his eyebrow at her but remained silent.

With that, she stood up and kissed Beef on the head, grabbed Wolf's hand and squeezed gently, then let it go and walked to the door. She opened the door to leave, but then paused and turned towards him, "Darnel's funeral is going to be in a couple weeks: Sunday the 30th, at 3 p.m. at the church, followed by the burial. Matt and I thought we'd take the burden off your shoulders and plan everything. It would mean a lot to me if you were there. Have a good day, Will." And with that, she was gone, closing the door behind her.

Wolf sat in his chair, taking in everything she had said to him. Why did she have to bring her God into this? God couldn't forgive a man like him. And even if He could, why would He? But she forgave him… he told her exactly what he had done last night, and she forgave him. Even comforted him! Who was this woman? What made her love the way she did? He had just met her, and she had taken care of him like she had known him for years. There was something special about this girl, about these people. He needed to talk to them again, to her again, and he knew exactly where she was going.

Wolf walked into the kitchen, grabbed a green apple, and picked up his keys. "Mount up, Beef," he said, as he walked to the front door. The little, fat beast immediately lifted his head from the couch, barked once, jumped down to the floor, and followed his master out to the truck. Wolf opened the driver side door, picked up the little white dog with a grunt, and put him up in the cab. Beef jumped into the passenger seat, wagged his tail, and snorted. Wolf chuckled and shook his head. "Yes, we're going to go see the pretty lady that kissed your head," he said to the dog. He climbed into the rig and started the engine, turning the volume dial on the stereo up, and driving away.

# Chapter 9

# The Protected

June 8th, 2013, 1:00 p.m. Wolf pulled into the church parking lot and shut off the engine. In front of him was a red Mustang with tape over the driver side tail light. Wolf felt a knot in his stomach. "Not here. Not her..." Wolf muttered to himself quietly. He didn't have any of his weapons on him; he had rushed out the door too fast. He whacked the steering wheel with his fist, "Think Wolf, think," he told himself almost frantically. Realization dawned on him: he looked in the back seat and saw a solid oak Louisville Slugger sitting on the floorboard. He and Darnel had gone to the batting cages three weeks earlier and he had left the bat in the backseat and forgot about it. Reaching over to the seat, he grabbed the bat and opened the door, stepping out and onto the pavement. He cracked the windows down, then turned off the truck, retrieving the keys. He pulled on the hood of his sweatshirt and tucked his dog tags under his shirt. "Stay in the truck, Beef," he said, then closed the door and made his way to the church.

As he approached the Mustang, he saw that nobody was inside it. He heard yelling from the church. Wolf sprinted to the double doors at the front of the building and slid in silently. As he stood in the foyer, he heard a man's voice pleading with somebody in the sanctuary. "Gentlemen, please! This is a church!" It was Matt.

"Oh, we know; we've just come to pay our respects to your slain attack dog. It's a shame that he had to be put down so young..." another voice sneered. Wolf kicked open the doors, revealing the sanctuary.

Two men were on either side of Matt. One of them had a gas can. The other man was smoking a cigarette. Matt was on his knees, bleeding from his left eyebrow. "Who is this, preacher man?" the man with the cigarette asked Matt.

Wolf noted that both men were armed and had no intention of stepping away from Matt unless he gave them a reason to. He gripped the bat a little tighter in his right hand. "Well," Wolf said, "at this moment, I would say a witness to arson and assault. Or is there more you would like on that rap sheet?"

The man with the cigarette pulled his firearm from his holster. The pastor reacted before Wolf could move, grabbing ahold of the man's arm, wrestling with him, keeping him from getting a clear shot. The other man dropped the gasoline can and pulled a large knife from his jacket, aiming to stab the pastor. Before he could lunge towards Matt, Wolf was already upon him. The solid oak Louisville Slugger came crashing down on the man's arm.

There was a loud crack as both the man's radius and ulna snapped in half on impact. He grabbed his arm, screaming in agony, dropping the knife to the floor. Wolf capitalized, driving the fat end of the bat into the man's left knee, crumpling him to the ground. He then drove his combat boot right to the man's teeth, busting eight of them, and rendering the man unconscious.

The gunman had been able to make room between himself and the pastor by head-butting Matt. The pastor stumbled back slightly and was rewarded with a mean left hook, causing him to crash back into a pew. Wolf charged the gunman, bat at the ready, when a shot rang out, grazing the flesh of Wolf's left forearm. He grunted and swung the bat, cracking it across the barrel of the gun, sending it soaring to the other side of the room. Dropping the bat, he let the momentum of the swing carry his right shoulder into the other man's chest. They both crashed over a pew and landed on the ground. Wolf was on his back with the attacker on top of him.

Wolf was on his guard, trying to defend the wild elbows and punches the man was throwing down on him. He was pinned between the pews, unable to put his Brazilian jiu-jitsu to full work. The man continued to rain down blows that were rendered ineffective as Wolf defended them all with his arms. His attacker scooped up his partner's large knife and reared up to stab Wolf in the chest. Before he could bring the blade down, something struck him in the side of the head, making him drop the knife. Wolf instantly threw his legs around the man's neck with his left leg behind his attacker's head and locked his left foot behind his right knee: executing a picture-perfect triangle choke. He squeezed as hard as he could, for what seemed like an eternity, before the man's body went limp.

Pushing the unconscious man off himself, Wolf got back up to his feet and sat in the pew. The pastor was leaning on the armrest of the pew across the aisle, the tip of the Louisville Slugger resting on the ground with the handle hanging loosely in his hand. Wolf looked over at him, both men panting as they tried to calm down their heartbeats. Wolf reached up and pulled off his hood. Both men just sat there, trying to catch their breath. Wolf broke the silence, "Forgive me, Father, for I have sinned."

Matt raised his eyebrows, bursting out laughing, shaking his head. After he caught his breath, he looked into Wolf's eyes. "It doesn't work like that, my friend. Gotta take it up with the Man upstairs. And it's Matt, remember?"

"Whatever you say, Reverend," Wolf responded.

Matt shook his head once more, then a look of curiosity passed his face. "How did you know that they were going to be here?"

"I didn't," Wolf answered. "I was looking for Jess when I saw the Mustang out front. Looked like trouble, so I grabbed my bat and ran in. Nice swing by the way."

Matt nodded, "Thanks."

"No problem."

"So... should we call the cops?" Matt asked.

Wolf shook his head. "Tyrone owns the police. I will call Detective Westbrooke. She is one of the good ones."

Matt nodded his head, "DJ respected her too. Have you taken over as an asset for DJ?"

"Not necessarily, no." Wolf answered, "I am more of a private investigator."

"I would lean more towards a vigilante," Matt responded.

Wolf chuckled, "Fair enough Father, fair enough."

Matt paused for a moment, calculating his words. "Just answer me this one question," he said finally, "Are you doing this for DJ, or yourself?"

"Neither," Wolf responded. "I'm doing this for the same reason Darnel defended this church. I'm protecting the lives of innocent people that can't protect themselves."

Matt nodded his head. "Well, usually I would preach that God says, 'Turn the other cheek.' Not only that, but I am obligated to turn you in to the authorities if I assume you're doing something outside the law... However, these filthy delinquents were aiming to burn down my church with me in it, before you showed up. So, as far as I am concerned, you are my new security liaison, and I am willing to hire you to make it official."

Wolf smiled. "Delinquents, huh? You sure that's a word you can use? Might need to rinse your mouth with holy water there, Reverend," he said with a wink.

Matt chuckled and shook his head, then his eyes widened in horror. "You're bleeding!" he exclaimed.

Wolf looked at his arm and shrugged, "It's just a scratch."

Matt stood up and looked a little closer at the wound, "I'm going to call Jess to stitch you up."

"Send her to my place; I'll be there in an hour. I have work to do." Wolf reached into his pocket and pulled out zip-ties. He bound both men's wrists and ankles together so that they could not escape. Wolf reached into one of the men's pockets and pulled out his car keys. "I'm going to bring their car back to them; you think you can watch them until the detective gets here?" The pastor nodded. "Good. Have Jess take my truck home if she can; Beef is waiting for me," he said, and handed the pastor the keys. Wolf walked outside into the muggy Denver air once again.

"Hey, Will," a voice said. Wolf turned to see the pastor standing at the front door of the church. "How far are you going to take this?"

Wolf took in a deep breath and let out a long sigh. "Father, these men killed my brother and the law isn't doing anything about it. If you were me, how far would you go?"

The pastor nodded, "I'll be praying for you, my friend." With that, he closed the door. Wolf got into the Mustang and drove out of the parking lot.

# Chapter 10

# The Warning

June 8th, 2013, 2:45 p.m. Wolf sat in the driver seat of the Mustang. He stared ahead, at the gated off house at the end of the street: Tyrone's house. He finished writing on a piece of paper he found in the glove box. The note read: *Admit to your crimes or there will be repercussions.* He put the note in the center console.

In the front passenger seat, sat a tire iron and a cinder block. Ice ran through his veins as he put the car into drive, keeping his foot on the brake. Taking the tire iron, he drove it through the gap in the steering wheel and wedged it up against the dashboard so that it would not slip out of place. Jiggling the steering wheel, he nodded his content as it refused to move from its place. He opened the door and put one foot onto the pavement. In so doing, he grabbed the cinder block and placed it onto the gas pedal, keeping his right foot firmly on the brake. The engine revved loudly as the tires spun. Wolf made sure that he was holding the door open wide with his left hand, and lunged out of the vehicle, spinning out of the way just in time, as the car sped away unmanned.

The car squealed its tires and careened down the road. The men standing on guard duty looked up to see the red sports car picking up speed, heading right at them. Watching, they recognized the car. Realizing that the vehicle was not slowing down, they opened fire before diving out of the way. They narrowly escaped the vehicle as it rammed through the front gate, sending broken debris into the front lawn of Tyrone's home. The seemingly possessed vehicle crumpled onto the metal gate and got itself pinned onto the brick wall opening, still spinning tires. The men ran around in a panic, trying to make sense of it all. Wolf smiled and walked towards the thrift shop a block away, where he used the payphone to call a cab and head home.

While in the cab, his phone began to buzz; he pulled it out of his pocket and answered, "Hello?"

A female voice that he recognized, answered him, "Hello, Will? This is Detective Kate Westbrooke. How are you doing?"

"I'm doing good, Detective; thanks for asking. How can I help you?" he asked.

"Call me Kate, Will," she said, "I just got a call from Darnel's pastor friend. Two of Tyrone's thugs were beat up and hogtied with zip-ties in his sanctuary. When I asked how he overpowered them, he said I would have to speak to his security liaison. Know anything about that?"

Wolf smirked, "Sounds like they couldn't handle the sermon."

She chuckled slightly but tried to hide it with a sigh, "Will, is there anything I need to know?"

"I can't say for certain. I've never been in a church long enough to hear a sermon before," he responded.

He heard her stifle another chuckle with a sigh, "I guess you wouldn't know about the attack on his men last night either then?" Wolf remained silent. "Will, you promised me evidence."

"Kate, you have two men caught attempting arson on a church and assaulting the pastor. How much more evidence do you need?" he asked.

"It would be a lot better with a statement from the so-called 'security liaison,'" she answered.

"When this is finished, I will give you any statement you need," Wolf said.

She sighed, "Okay, Will. Be careful."

"As a cinder block in a Mustang," Wolf responded.

"Wait, what?" she asked.

"Never mind. I will check in when I have more for you. Goodbye, Kate."

"Goodbye, Will," and then the call ended.

Twenty minutes later, Wolf paid the taxi driver with cash and went inside where he was greeted by an overly excited Beef, snorting and wagging his little, fat rear. Wolf stooped down and began scratching his head and under his chin. "Hi Beef, good boy. Ah yeah, good boy Beef."

He looked up to meet the gaze of Jessica, looking frazzled but beautiful as always. She smiled at him and then looked at the blood dripping from his left hand to the hardwood floor. "Let's get you stitched up," she said, as she walked towards his kitchen. He followed her in. "Can you take off your sweatshirt?" she asked. Wolf nodded and pulled it off, grimacing as it went over his wound, and throwing it into his laundry room to the right of the kitchen.

She had him stand over the sink so that he wouldn't bleed on the floor or cupboards. A suture needle with thread, disinfecting alcohol, gauze, and tape sat on the countertop. She had him rest his left arm on the counter directly next to the sink, in the light, so that she would get a good look at his forearm. The wound had cut laterally across his arm and wasn't too deep. She looked closely, examined the area around the wound for a few seconds, and then seemed to get sidetracked rubbing her hand over the scarred tissue on his arm. Her eyes grew wider and wider as she realized the extent of the burns. Finally, she looked him in the eyes, tears forming in her own. "What happened to you?"

Wolf hesitated. He didn't like remembering what had happened. These scars of his were a daily reminder of a nightmare that he felt would never leave the central cortex of his brain. The pit in his stomach he had since he saw his friend dead on that table, deepened into a chasm. Realizing his hesitation, he cleared his throat, "I was blown up by an RPG. Darnel saved my life… it was our last mission… we were the only survivors."

She looked back down, focusing on his arm and wiping away her tears, "Luckily you were only grazed. Don't have to dig out the bullet; good…" she muttered, almost to herself, as she studied his wound.

"Are you explaining the pros of a bullet grazing over a bullet wound, or are you just reminding yourself?" Wolf asked her with a slight chuckle. She looked up to meet his gaze and he smiled at her.

She blushed and looked down at his forearm, "Maybe both. I have to sterilize the wound. Put your arm over the sink, please." He did as he was told. "This is probably going to hurt; I forgot to bring a numbing agent or pain killers."

Wolf just shrugged. "Better you didn't. Addict; remember?" he reminded her. She nodded, though Wolf had a sneaking suspicion that she had something in opposition to say on his comment.

She opened the bottle of alcohol and paused for a second; she took a breath and gripped his hand. She then poured it onto Wolf's wound and winced as soon as it made contact, as if she had felt the sting. Wolf didn't even flinch. She looked up at him with those magnificent eyes and with genuine shock and asked, "Did that even hurt?"

Wolf shrugged, "I felt it."

She stared at him in amazement. She lifted an eyebrow and poured more onto the wound, staring at his face as she did it. Once again, he didn't react. "Nothing?" she asked in amazement.

He smiled at her, "Nope." She stared at him for a few more moments and then started wiping the wound with a sterile cloth. She grabbed the needle and began to sew the lips of the wound together. Once again, Wolf didn't react as she worked on his arm; he just watched her handiwork.

Clearing her throat, she began a conversation as she focused on what she was doing. "So, Matt told me that you stopped a couple of Tyrone's goons from burning down the church today. He says you were like his guardian angel, swooping in at the perfect moment."

Wolf smirked, "Funny, he told Kate I was his new security liaison." Jessica shook her head, smiling slightly. After a short pause, he added, "I'm far from an angel. Besides, the priest got a few hits himself."

He caught her smile at that, "He's not a priest, Will. He's a pastor."

"Well, whatever he is, he must have been a part of the Catholic schoolboy t-ball league or something. Had a nice swing on him, caught that guy right in the sweet spot."

She smiled again, trying not to laugh, "Once again, he's a pastor. He's not Catholic." She shook her head. "As for the angel thing, we all have our demons, Will. None of us are perfect."

"Some of us are less perfect than others..." Wolf responded. "You don't know half the things I have done, Jess, how many lives I have took."

She looked up at his face for a few moments, making sure he was staring directly into her eyes, "Your past doesn't define you, Will: it refines you." Then she looked back down at his forearm, finishing the sutures. She put a sterile dressing over it and taped it down. "You might not want to use that arm too much, I'd hate to see you rip out those stitches."

Wolf smiled, "Well, if I don't rip them out every once in a while, I won't have an excuse to see you..."

She looked up at him and blushed, "I um... I'm going to go help Matt clean up the church; do you want to come with me?"

"I'd love to," he answered, "but I have some recon to do."

She nodded her head, "Just try not to get killed, okay?"

"Marines don't die, ma'am, we go to hell and regroup," he replied.

She stared at him with a very serious look in her eyes. "Please," she said bluntly.

Wolf nodded his head, "I'll be careful."

She nodded at him then walked over to his freezer. Taking out a bag of frozen peas, she wrapped it in a hand towel and brought it over to him, gently laying it over the bandage. "Ice for twenty minutes, then do your recon. It will keep the swelling down," she ordered. Wolf nodded and she smiled at him. She leaned forward and kissed him on the forehead. "I'll call you tomorrow," she said, and walked towards the door.

Wolf stared blankly for a moment, processing what just happened. Then Wolf remembered how she got there. "Jess, wait," he struggled out through the thumping in his chest from his rapid heartbeat. Wolf cleared his throat, "I uh... I'm your ride..."

She stood in the door for a second as realization dawned on her face. "Right, I forgot I drove your truck here," she said blushing, "Nice rig by the way."

He smiled, "You haven't seen anything yet. Wait here."

Wolf walked into the garage, past his workout equipment, and opened the door, revealing the once again covered Chevelle. He pulled off the tarp and got into the car, pushing the button opening the garage door and then fired her up. Jess was standing on the front porch with her mouth on the floor. He rolled down the window and hollered out at her, "Are you going to stand there with your jaw on the floor, or are you going to get in?"

Jessica climbed into the passenger seat. "Where did you get this?" she asked.

"It was Darnel's," he said, rubbing the steering wheel. "He built her from the ground up; she was his baby. Driving her makes me feel like he's still here with me."

"I never saw him drive her," she said.

Wolf nodded his head, "He only drove her around the block a few times a month to keep her going. He almost totaled her when he was drunk one night, so she spent most of the time in the garage. Washed and polished her regularly."

Jessica nodded her head. "Well, she's gorgeous."

*She's not the only one*, Wolf thought to himself, as he stared at Jessica for a long, hard second. Then, clearing his throat once more, he put the Chevelle in gear and rumbled down the road. They talked about life, family, and fond memories of Darnel until he rolled up to the church twenty minutes later and Jessica got out of the car.

"Be safe tonight, Will," she said, as she closed the door. Wolf watched her as she walked away, entranced once more. Then he put the Chevelle back in gear and sped away.

# Chapter 11

# The Aspect

June 8th, 2013, 10:00 p.m. Wolf sat parked in an alley around the corner from Tyrone's house. He had a comms unit sitting on the dashboard; a laptop and a journal sat on the front passenger seat. He reached over and grabbed an antenna with a wire attached to it. He put his mask on and slipped the antenna into the inside pocket of his jacket. He shut the door to the car and locked it with the key. Slipping into the shadows of the buildings around him, Wolf made his way back to the tree on the corner of the wall. Most of the men were trying to figure out how to get the crumpled-up beer can of a Ford Mustang removed from the clutches of their severely mangled gate. This left the wall unguarded.

Wolf ran up the side of the tree, just as he had done the night before. However, when he landed, he immediately had to dive back into the shadows as a guard approached. Wolf remained completely still against the wall, the darkness of night covering his position. The man walked only a few feet from Wolf. He paused for a moment, pulled out a cigarette, lit it, and then kept walking. Wolf remained still for a couple minutes more, making sure the man was completely out of sight.

When the coast was clear, Wolf made a break for the side of the house; there was a power box with a padlock on the exterior wall, wiring power to the house. Pulling out his lock-pick tools, Wolf unfastened the padlock and opened the small door. Inside, he found cables. Shifting through them, he found the cable he was looking for: the landline. Next to that was a thicker cable that made Wolf smile under his mask, *Seems our drug lord has cameras inside.* He snipped into the wire, attached the antenna device and powered it on, then shut the door, refastening the padlock. He heard a noise coming from around the corner, so he slipped to the back of the house. They had moved the dumpster away from the wall after his last escape; he would have to find another way over the wall.

Seeing nothing to climb onto, Wolf sprinted to the corner of the walls, launching straight up into the air. He planted his left boot on the left part of the corner, pushing off to plant his right boot on the opposing right wall, and grasping the top of the wall with both hands. Then he pulled himself over the wall and into the darkness of the road once more. He snuck quietly back to the Chevelle, turning on the laptop. As it booted up, he pulled a flash drive from the center console and plugged it into one of the USB ports on the computer.

There were four boxes on the screen, each with its own image that changed every ninety seconds. The top two displayed the living room from different angles; the bottom two were of the kitchen and the front porch. The images shifted, revealing the exterior of the house. The first two were of the porch: one on the main door and the other pointed towards the yard. The other two captured the main gate. Both were of different vantage points, focusing on the broken entryway and the crumpled, red sports car permanently parked in the front end of the house. Wolf clicked on that one, keeping it from changing. The other three shifted to reveal an office, the inside of the garage, and the kitchen. Just before the screen was about to change, two men walked into the office. Wolf quickly clicked on the box, keeping it from shifting once more. The other two were still cycling through the cameras in the house.

Wolf observed the screen, silently watching who was walking into the rooms. He took note of what weapons they were carrying and what their chain of command was. The comms unit was giving him an audio feed to each room. It was set to cycle to the next room automatically every ninety seconds, just like the video, unless he manually channeled it to a certain room.

He focused in on a fit, young black man, wearing pinstripe slacks and a silk blue dress shirt. Everything was wrinkle-free, pressed to perfection: the clothes of an accomplished businessman. He was sitting behind his desk in his high back chair, seeming unamused by the men sitting across the desk from him. His posture was stoic as he sat silently glaring at the men. One of them was researching contractors, on his phone, to fix the front gate.

"When will the car be removed from my gate?" the man in the high back chair asked, in a calm voice that was almost chilling.

"Sir, we don't have the equipment necessary to remove the car," one of the men answered.

"Get the equipment then," Tyrone answered.

"That's easier said than done, sir. We need to put in for a licensed professional. Can take maybe three to four weeks," the man responded.

Tyrone leaned forward in his chair. He stared at both men intensely, "You have four hours. Grab a chop saw from the van in the garage. Clean it off so there is no residue left on the gate, then go cut it out." Both men looked at each other, then at Tyrone, and back at each other. Tyrone slammed the desk with his fist and both men jumped up and ran out of his office, shutting the door behind them. Tyrone let out an audible sigh and leaned back into his chair.

Then he reached into the top drawer of the desk and pulled out two notes. "For the sake of justice…" he read quietly to himself. "What justice is it that you seek?" Tyrone got up from his desk and tacked both notes into a corkboard wall. He studied the notes for a moment, silently. The silence was disturbed by a soft buzzing sound. Tearing his attention from the corkboard, Tyrone slipped his hand into his jacket pocket and retrieved a cell phone. "Detective," he said in a stern voice.

Wolf turned up the volume of the laptop and could make out the hesitant voice of a man coming from the other end of the phone. "Sir, Jacobs and Simms are in custody for attempted arson and battery. Neither of them are talking, but they are both pretty banged up. The preacher said something about having a new security liaison but would not give any information of who that individual may be, or where to find him. There is enough evidence against your men to put them away for a long time, with or without this security liaison's statement. For all we know, preacher man was by himself."

"Don't be a fool, Detective. We both know the preacher lacks the backbone to fight back," Tyrone responded

"Seems you don't know the preacher too well... Good," Wolf said to himself.

Tyrone continued, "Someone intercepted Jacobs and Simms. Someone highly trained that knows how to disappear. I believe it may be the same man that attacked my men on the porch and sent another to the emergency room. Did you get anything from the security feed I sent?"

A sigh emanated from the other side of the phone, "Yeah, you are probably right. I got the feed. Whoever that guy was, he's a pro. The camera only got a few glimpses of him, but nothing substantial. Even if they had got a good look, he wore a mask and didn't leave anything behind. He scooped up the brass from the rounds he shot before taking off. Never seen anything like it... besides the military guy you gunned down a few days back."

Wolf's eyes widened, "Got him..."

Tyrone remained calm, however. "Detective, I don't have the faintest idea what you are going on about. However, if I did, I would caution you to keep your assumptions to yourself. You aren't paid to be sloppy. What makes you think I would allow myself to be?"

"Knew it wouldn't be that easy," Wolf said after a short sigh.

The detective on the other end seemed to panic, "Sorry sir, I did not mean anything by it. Must have been thinking of another case. My mistake."

"Good," Tyrone said in a chilling voice, "Don't let it happen again. Remember, that badge can't protect you from me."

"Yes sir, sorry sir," the unsteady voice of the dirty detective answered. "I may have something for you though."

"Carry on," the chilling voice responded.

"Well… it may be nothing or it may be something, but… I have been going through the case files where you were the suspect and one is missing."

"Which one?" Tyrone asked sternly.

"The guard dog from the church," the detective answered.

"I thought you closed the case," Tyrone responded.

"I did," the detective answered with obvious panic in his voice. "But the file is missing."

"Don't mistake my calm voice for patience, Detective Bishop. Who was the investigation lead?" Tyrone stated sternly. Wolf wrote the name *Bishop* in the notepad he had on the dash.

"Westbrooke," Bishop answered.

Tyrone kicked a chair across the room, making it crash into the opposing wall. "I thought you handled that situation."

"She's stubborn, sir. She isn't easily persuaded," Bishop responded.

Tyrone gritted his teeth, "Persuade her, or I will clean up your mistake. Understood?"

"Yes sir," Bishop responded instantly.

"Good. While you are at it, find out all you can about the guard dog. I think there may be something there," the angry drug lord said.

"Consider it done," Bishop responded.

"I will consider nothing until I see facts," Tyrone said, then hung up the phone. "Imbecile." He then stormed out of the office and toward the front gate.

Wolf's phone began buzzing; the caller wasn't from his contact list. He answered it to hear the voice of the pastor through the speakers. "Will?" he asked.

"Reverend?" Wolf answered.

The pastor sighed, "I was wondering if you could come by the church. We just got done with our men's group and I was hoping you and I could talk a little bit."

Wolf hesitated. "I'm kind of in the middle of something, Reverend."

There was a long pause on the other end of the line. "Will, they threatened my family…"

Wolf stared out the windshield, into the dark night, "I'll be there in ten minutes." Wolf hung up the phone and started the Chevelle, putting her in gear. Releasing the clutch, he burned rubber out of the dark alley and into the road, roaring down the street. Anger coursed through his veins, causing his heart to pound loudly in his ears.

He flew down the streets of Denver, seeming to catch every green light on his way to the church. As soon as he pulled into the driveway, Wolf immediately saw the pastor waiting out front. Removing his mask and gloves, Wolf placed them in his jacket pocket. The engine clicked off as he pulled out the keys, placing them in his front, right pant pocket after locking the door behind himself. The pastor had already made his way towards Wolf. They shook hands and walked side by side into the building.

When they were in the sanctuary, Matt made his way to the front and sat on the edge of the stage. Wolf sat in the pew across from him, waiting for the preacher. After a long silence, the pastor finally spoke, looking down at his feet the whole time. "They threatened my wife and kids today, Will. They were at the park... my boys were playing on the swings and two of Tyrone's goons walked up to them. My wife went to intervene, but Tyrone's right-hand man, Damien, cut her off. He told her he had a message for me. He said I had two options: leave or pay the price of admission. Then he tried to touch my wife. Luckily people were around, so when she slapped his hand, he backed off..." Wolf sat in silence. "They threatened to burn my boys alive and make my wife and I watch." His hands began to shake with anger. "He left and motioned for his men to follow him. My wife ran over to our boys on the swing and saw that the men had given one of them a matchbook, the other lighter fluid."

Wolf tightened his fists. The pastor's body was rigid. His hands still shook with rage. Finally, he looked up, meeting Wolf's gaze. His eyes were red and puffy; he had been crying. "Will... they threatened my family."

"They won't get the chance to act on that threat," Wolf said coldly.

Matt sucked in a deep breath and let it out before cocking his head to the side. "You know, Darnel said the same thing to me when they threatened to burn down the church. They killed him that same night... what makes you any different?"

Wolf clenched his jaw. "I have nothing to lose. There's no redemption for a man like me."

"That's not true, Will; there is always redeeming grace, for all men," the pastor said.

Wolf's voice was cold as ice as his face turned into a sheet of granite. "I'm not a man; not anymore."

Matt lowered his head, not having the energy to argue. "Well, whatever you're going to do, do it fast. Because all you've done so far is poke the bear, and he isn't happy about it."

"You saw what I did to two of them with a baseball bat. You really think I only carry a stick?" Wolf retorted.

"What if they kill you, Will?"

"They'll be doing me a favor," he responded, as he shifted his gaze away from the pastor.

Matt hit the stage with his fist. "See, right there. That's what scares me."

"What?"

"You want to die. You're hoping for it. What good would that do?" Silence momentarily filled the room.

The pastor stared at Wolf, he could tell that Matt was not going to let this question remain unanswered. He took a deep breath then let it out slowly before responding. "Just because I wish for death, doesn't mean I am willing to go down without a fight. And I would love to see if any of them are man enough for the job."

With that, Wolf stood up and began to walk away. "Will," the pastor said. The marine paused, then turned to look at him. "You have to survive this. I know a way for you to have your redemption. You can be reborn; have all your demons and sins washed clean from you."

Wolf turned his head slightly so he could talk over his shoulder, "If by some miracle I survive this, I'll be needing a pastor on Sunday mornings to show me the ropes." With that, he walked out of the building. Crossing the parking lot, he took out his keys and opened the door to the Chevelle. After a quick scope of his surroundings, he climbed into the car and called Detective Westbrooke. After three rings, she answered the phone.

"Will?"

"Go to a motel; use cash. Watch your six. Tyrone's been tipped off; he knows you have the file," he said quickly.

"Understood," she answered, and hung up the phone.

Wolf started the car, put it in gear, and drove back to his house. Pulling the Chevelle into the garage, he went inside after making sure the automatic door shut. This was going to be a long night: there was cancer to remove.

# Wolf Jackson

# Chapter 12

# The Invasion

June 9th, 2013, 12:00 a.m. Wolf was in his room. A duffle lay open on his bed as he put shotgun shells, mags for his guns, and extra ammo into the bag. The doors to the wardrobe were wide open: all the guns were laid out on his bed, each one fully loaded. Wolf walked over to the wardrobe and pushed on the bottom board, causing it to lift up on one side. He grabbed it with his free hand and pulled the board out, revealing ten bricks of plastic explosives with a remote detonator, four claymores, and ten flashbang grenades.

Forget gathering evidence; the police couldn't help him now. This monster was going to walk away from threatening an innocent man's family. Killing Darnel was bad enough, but threatening the lives of children with something as sadistic as burning them to death, was beyond mere prison time. This had just become a death sentence.

Wolf grabbed all the explosives and placed them in the duffle bag. He put his shotgun and M4 into the bag as well, then returned to the wardrobe to collect the magazines for the M4 and the shells for the shotgun. His phone buzzed; pulling it from of his pants pocket, he opened a text from Kate Westbrooke: *They know your address.*

Beef began to growl; the hairs on the back of his neck rose up. Wolf stared at him intently and listened... There was a soft creak from the front room. Wolf snapped his finger towards the bed and the little white dog dove underneath it. Clicking off the light, Wolf jumped into the wardrobe, leaving the duffle bag on the bed.

Wolf heard movement by the doorway. Silently he waited, keeping his breath quiet and calm. The figure of a man skulked into the room; Wolf could tell that he was carrying a shotgun. He was looking around, scanning everything. The man leaned down to look underneath the bed. Wolf drew his combat knife and clicked the back wall of the wardrobe with his blade three times. The man paused and stood up, turning towards the sound. Wolf slowly squatted down, planting his right foot on the back wall. The man took a step towards the wardrobe with the shotgun trained on the double doors. Taking his left hand off the barrel of the shotgun, right hand on the trigger, the man reached out to rip open the door. Wolf exploded out of the wardrobe, catching the man with his shoulder in the chest, knocking the wind out of him and taking him to the ground. Sound turned into a deafening ring as the gun went off just to the right of Wolf's head. He wrestled with the gunman as the assailant struggled back to his feet. Wolf stopped trying to block out the left arm, giving himself space to swipe upward with his knife, slicing the other man in the forearm. The man retaliated, releasing the stock of the gun with his injured arm, and swung a wild haymaker. Wolf ducked it and slipped behind his opponent. Shots rang out from the doorway as somebody fired blindly into the room. Wolf grabbed his assailant's vest, keeping him between himself and the doorway. His human meat shield collapsed, and Wolf rolled silently into the shadows.

Another gunman with a pistol walked into the room slowly. He grabbed the man on the floor and flipped him over to reveal his comrade with four rounds caught in his Kevlar. He was gasping for air. He released him to the floor and clicked on the flashlight. Wolf did not have time to evade the beam of light as it quickly swept the room revealing his hiding place. The man raised his firearm then suddenly lurched backwards in pain. The gun went off, putting a hole in the wall just above Wolf's head. Wolf saw a small burly animal attached to the man's calf: Beef. Wolf lunged from his hiding place, crossed the bedroom and scooped the other man's shotgun off the ground. The assailant brought his pistol down towards Beef. He was not fast enough. Wolf swung the butt of the shotgun like a baseball bat and cracked the man across the jaw, crumpling him to the floor in a heap. Even after the man collapsed, Beef refused to release his leg. Wolf retrieved the flashlight and shined it on the man to reveal a Kevlar vest with *POLICE* spelled in white across the top. *Bishop,* Wolf thought.

Reaching into the duffle bag, Wolf pulled out a few of the flashbang grenades and retrieved his M&P .45 ACP with four fully loaded mags, tucking the gun in the holster on the small of his back and the mags in his left rear pocket. He kicked the other man's gun across the room and motioned for Beef to stay where he was. The ringing in his good ear began to clear up; he could hear footsteps from the living room. Cocking the shotgun back slightly, Wolf could see that it was loaded with slugs instead of shells. He released the action and reset the round. Taking the three flashbangs in his left hand, he pulled the pins out all at once, with his teeth, and threw the canisters into the front room, ducking back behind the door before they went off.

The canisters exploded, momentarily paralyzing the equilibrium of the two assailants who had been waiting for him to exit the room. Sprinting forward, Wolf hit one of them in the face with the butt of the shotgun. He dropped the other one with his left elbow, driving it into the man's temple. Another assailant appeared to his left, down the hallway. Wolf quickly turned and fired his shotgun, catching the man in the vest, launching him up against the wall and to the floor, gasping for air. The large glass window to his right, in the kitchen, shattered. He vaulted over the couch and ran up the stairs to the second story. The intruder from the kitchen attempted to chase after him but was also caught in the chest with a slug from the shotgun.

Wolf stood behind the wall at the top of the stairs, listening for more intruders. All he could hear was moans from the men he had incapacitated. After a moment, he decided to head down the stairs, hesitating momentarily as he saw that the door across from him was no longer padlocked. He began to walk towards it, but the doorbell rang. "Will! Will! It's Kate! Open up!" Wolf went to the door, Beef coming from his hiding place and following close behind his master.

# Chapter 13

# The Scalpel

June 9th, 2013, 12:30 a.m. Wolf sat at the kitchen table with Detective Kate Westbrooke. Four uniformed policemen were taking pictures of the crime scene. Wolf had let Kate in after the attack; she immediately called for back-up and an ambulance for the assailants while Wolf tied their hands with zip-ties. He had hidden the duffle bag in the room upstairs before the boys in blue arrived, pausing to see that the room had been lived in. The bed was made, but there were dirty clothes in the hamper and a fan had been left on. "The secrets never stop, do they brother?" Wolf asked, as if his friend was still there with him. He let out a sigh and shut the door, then returned to Kate downstairs just as the police arrived with EMT's.

Kate sat at the table with Wolf when the cops began to question him. "Sir," the younger policeman began, "to the best of your ability, could you tell us what happened."

Wolf shrugged, "I was in my bedroom with Beef when he began to growl. That is when I heard footsteps coming from the front room and took a tactical position in the wardrobe. I overtook the first assailant, slicing him with my knife—"

"The knife you still have on your possession?" the cop interrupted.

"Irrelevant," Wolf said bluntly.

"Well, it's not; we may need it for evidence."

"Wrong again."

"Sir, if you want to press charges, we are going to need the knife as evidence."

"Who said anything about pressing charges?" Wolf asked. "Kate, did you hear anything about pressing charges?"

"Not that I heard, Will," Kate responded.

The cop was befuddled, "But… Sir, these are off duty police officers that attacked you in your home… why wouldn't you press charges?"

Wolf stared at him blankly. "Because I don't need to for them to be prosecuted. You just said they were off duty cops that broke into my home and assaulted me. All you need is my statement, not for me to press charges. The oath they took when they became policemen will take care of that."

The cop shifted the weight on his feet, "That may be true, but don't you want them to serve as much time as possible?" the cop asked.

"They are crooked cops going to prison… they won't last more than a couple months," Wolf said bluntly. "Now, do you want my statement or not?"

The cop sighed, scribbled some notes, then motioned for Wolf to continue. "As I was saying, I overtook the first assailant and Beef bit the second. I cracked him in the face with the butt of the shotgun. I used stun grenades on the two in the front room, dropping one with my elbow and the other with the shotgun I stole from the first assailant. Fifth assailant took a slug to the vest, sixth received the same on the stairs. And that's when Kate showed up."

After scribbling some more notes, the officer turned to Kate, "Detective, can you tell me why you came over?"

Kate just stared at him for a moment, "His roommate was my friend. I came to offer my condolences."

"Any other reason?" the cop asked.

"You have a habit of asking questions that are none of your business," Wolf said. The cop just stared at him. "Are we done here?"

The officer let out another sigh, "One more thing. How did you know that they were off duty cops and not just undercover?"

"You ever enter a building without stating you are the police, then commanding the assailant to come out with their hands up?" Wolf asked.

"No sir, we have a protocol to follow," the cop answered.

"Exactly," Wolf said.

The cop sighed, "I don't understand it. You had six trained men come into your home late at night, with weapons and body armor. Any normal person would hide and call the cops, but you take them down with a knife, stun grenades, and a stolen shotgun. Is that right?"

Wolf stared at him for a long hard moment, "First of all, the shotgun was borrowed. I gave it back. Second, the detective here called you at 0005; you arrived at 0015. If that isn't good enough for you, try this: I took out six men in one hundred and sixty-three seconds. Didn't need you."

The officer shifted his feet, "I don't think you understand how close you were to losing your life tonight. These men were cops, two of them former military."

"Sounds like they needed more training," Wolf said bluntly. "We done?"

"Well sir, we have all we need. We may call for you to testify against them in court, but other than that, have a safe night. Maybe get some plywood for that window."

"Thank you, officer," Wolf said, and all four uniformed men left. He turned to Kate, "I don't think he will call me for a second date."

She shook her head while smiling and asked, "You good?"

Wolf shrugged, "Might have ruptured an eardrum, but I will be fine." He leaned down and scratched Beef's head. "It's not going to be safe for you to go to work for a while, Kate. Might be best you get out of town."

Kate tapped the table with her finger a few times, "I have to work, Will. That's not an option."

He stood up and walked over to the counter, filled the coffee pot with water, then poured it into the silo. Placing a filter in the top, he took out the bag of beans from a cupboard, as well as the grinder. Kate waited patiently at the table as Wolf ground the beans and poured them into the coffee maker before hitting *brew*. As the machine gurgled and steamed, he watched the coffee begin to pour through the top of the pot. "You off the clock tonight, Detective?" he asked.

Kate kind of raised an eyebrow. "Yes, I am."

Wolf shifted his feet, "I have intel for you, but you can't use it as evidence."

"Okay… Why can't I use it?"

Wolf slid open a drawer and pulled it out of the track. Placing it on the counter, he reached inside to the empty space and retrieved his laptop. He reached into the gap once more, worked at something for a moment, and then produced the flash drive with a piece of tape attached to it. He brought both over to the table and turned on the laptop. Plugging in the flash drive, he pulled up the file he was looking for. He clicked on it twice, pulling up the video from earlier that night and fast-forwarding to the part when Tyrone was speaking on the phone to Bishop. Turning the screen towards Kate, he walked away to let her watch it, as he went over to fill up two coffee cups. Sipping on one, he brought the other to the table for Kate.

She sat at the table watching the screen, hearing the conversation between the crime boss and the detective on the other end. When Bishop's name was mentioned, she clenched her fists and began to shake. After a long moment, she looked Wolf in the eye, "Bishop is my boss, Will."

Wolf nodded his head, "I figured as much. That's why you have to skip town."

She shook her head, "If I do that, he will know that I am onto him. I need to be close to him so I can try to find a way to bury him." Wolf nodded his understanding, and they both sipped their coffee in silence. Kate was the one to finally speak. "Will, you're right, I can't use these feeds. Not without a warrant. Is there anything you can give me?"

He sipped his coffee and thought for a moment. He raised his good eyebrow as realization dawned on him, "Maybe." Wolf thought for a moment. "Bishop like to drink?"

"Yeah, he's at Finley's almost every night. Why?" she responded. "Is he there tonight?"

"Well, tonight is his night off, so I would assume so. Why?"

"I have a plan," he said calmly.

Kate nodded her head and continued to sip her cup of coffee. "It's not that I don't trust you, Will, but you have had a lot of crazy plans lately. Are you sure this is a good idea?" she asked.

"They threatened Matt's wife and kids. They are good people. Even if I wasn't sure about this, I would have to try."

Kate nodded her agreement and finished the cup. "Just be careful; Bishop is… jumpy," she said. Then she stood up and they walked together to the front door.

Wolf paused with his hand on the handle, "Do you have any clean cops that can watch the preacher's house tonight?"

Kate nodded, "I'll see what I can do. Stay safe, Will." He nodded his head and pulled open the door so she could leave.

Wolf looked over at the broken window to the left of the kitchen. "Oh yeah, I am real good and safe…" he said under his breath. After finishing his coffee, he got up from the table and went into the garage where he found two eight-foot 2x4's and a four-foot by eight-foot sheet of plywood. Using some screws and a DEWALT impact driver, Wolf laid the plywood across the shattered window and sealed it up tight with the 2x4's. He stepped back and shrugged at the patch job. Beef was standing on the back of the couch next to him, also staring at the boards. "Not Fort Knox, but it will have to do." Beef *gruffed* his agreement. Wolf pat his companion's head and scratched behind his ears real quick.

Putting the tools away, he went to the wardrobe and grabbed his leather jacket. Slipping it on, he walked back through the front room and retrieved the flash drive. He told Beef to stay and walked back into the garage to the Chevelle. Opening the garage door, he hopped into the car, started her up, and pulled out of the driveway.

Thirty minutes later, he pulled into Finley's parking lot, pulling into a dark corner by the back alley. Kate had sent him a photo of Detective Bishop so that he could identify him in the bar. Wolf was now looking at the picture of a slightly overweight, middle-aged man with a receding hairline. He wore big coke bottle glasses, with a neatly trimmed goatee. Just by looking at the picture, Wolf could tell that the man was a heavy drinker and a smoker. More than likely, he would be drinking alone. He got out of the car and opened the trunk, retrieving a black baseball cap. Slipping the cap on, he pulled the bill down to slightly conceal his marred face.

Wolf pulled a small bottle of Ipecac out of his pocket; he had retrieved it from the medicine cabinet on his way out the door. The clear bottle revealed a transparent, syrup-like liquid that induces vomiting and is mostly used for people who have overdosed on medications. Darnel had kept it on hand in case of a medical emergency as they both had to take sleep-aids. Both odorless and tasteless, Spec-Ops had been using Ipecac for years to abduct high-value targets as the abductee would have the medicine slipped into their drink when they weren't looking. When they would run to the bathroom or somewhere outside to vomit, the agents would make their move. The agents were trained to either pretend to help or simply whisk the target away, never to be heard from again.

Wolf and Darnel had been a part of such missions in the past. The results could be messy and less than pleasant, but effective. He noted the unmarked police cruiser five spaces to the right of the Chevelle. *Well, at least someone important is here*, he thought. He opened the medicine bottle and tore off the seal before recapping it and sliding it into his pocket. Stepping out of the car, he walked into the bar.

Wolf found Bishop pretty much right away: he was at a barstool by himself, watching the bartender whenever she bent over. He was sluggish and had trouble staying on the stool. Wolf was willing to bet that Bishop had already consumed too much alcohol for the night. But still, the bartender kept serving him, apparently used to this kind of behavior. Rounding the room, Wolf stuck to the shadows, finding a corner booth near the back. Some college kids were playing pool to his left, about ten feet behind Bishop. Sitting silently, Wolf watched as they attempted to knock the billiard balls into the holes. They'd had some to drink as well, giving Wolf exactly what he needed.

The shooter had his back to Wolf, trying to angle the cue just right. Just as he tried to hit the ball, Wolf tipped the pool cue up. The tip of the cue hit the bottom of the ball and launched it into the air. It landed right in Bishop's drink, splashing all over him and shattering the cup. He turned toward the kids, "Watch it punk!" he yelled.

"Calm down, old man," one of the kids said.

Bishop moved his coat back to show his shiny badge and a gun on his right hip. "No," he said, "you calm down and go home." The kids put the pool cues away, voicing their frustration loudly, and left the bar as Bishop shook the alcohol off his hands angrily.

Wolf made his move: he walked up to the bar with his head dipped slightly forward so the bill of the cap cast a shadow on his face. He sat on the stool next to Bishop, as the bartender wiped up the alcohol and tried to clear the broken glass. "Here," Wolf said, keeping the left side of his face from Bishop's view, "let me buy you another." He slapped down a twenty on the bar. "Hello, miss. One ginger ale and a uh..." he said motioning to Bishop.

Bishop stared at him for a moment. "Shot of Jack Daniels," Bishop answered.

Wolf looked over at the bartender. "Ginger ale and shot of Jack. Thank you."

"Thanks," Bishop said in a suspicious tone.

Wolf shrugged, "Anything for a police officer. Thank you for your service."

Bishop seemed to loosen up. "It's Detective, actually, and it's my pleasure."

Wolf nodded and waited for their drinks in silence, making sure to keep his chin slightly tucked to his chest. Both drinks arrived and were placed in front of the two men. "Thank you," Wolf said to the bartender, lifting his head slightly to acknowledge her; she smiled and went back to polishing cups. Wolf picked up his ginger ale and turned to walk away, catching the cue ball that had fallen to the floor, with his toe, making it roll three stools to the right of Bishop. "Say," he said pausing momentarily, "you don't know where that cue ball went, do you? Was thinking of hitting a few rounds myself."

Bishop began looking down below the bar, to the right. Seeing it under a stool, he nodded his head. "Yeah, let me grab it for you," he said, then bent over to reach for it. Wolf quickly dumped the contents of the bottle into the whiskey and slipped it back into his pocket before the detective saw it. Bishop sat back up and handed him the cue ball.

Wolf took it from him. "Much obliged," he said, then took his ginger ale and posted up at the pool table. The detective raised his glass toward him and nodded; Wolf reciprocated with his own glass. Both men took a drink. Wolf lowered his glass and smiled to himself as he began to rack the balls. He took a pool cue and began to play a game of pool by himself. Bishop knocked back his shot and ordered another drink; five minutes later, he vomited on the bar counter.

"Hey!" the bartender shouted, "Go out back if you're going to do that!"

Bishop covered his mouth and ran out the back door; Wolf continued to play pool and sip on his ginger ale. The detective walked back in, five minutes later, only to run back outside. Wolf finished his game and his ginger ale, then went out the front door. He rounded back to his Chevelle and saw the detective vomiting in the alleyway. The marine walked up to the sick man, "Hey, you alright there, Detective?"

Bishop waved a hand at him and tried to say something. Before the word could pass his lips, he turned and vomited yet again. Wolf reached out and pat his back with his right hand like one would to a small child who was getting sick. With his left hand, he reached into the coat pocket of the detective, pickpocketing his keys and his firearm, taking advantage of Bishop's situation.

Wolf left him alone and walked over to the unmarked cruiser out front. It was the standard, dark, royal blue Ford Fusion used by detectives, complete with comms, scanner, mounted laptop, and plexiglass divider between the front and back seat. He unlocked it with the keys and climbed into the vehicle. Wolf opened the laptop and powered it on. The device was password protected; Wolf remembered seeing Bishop's badge back in the bar: *CPB2546*. He typed in the numbers and unlocked the laptop. Pulling out the flash drive, he plugged it into the USB port and dragged the file from the video feed of Tyrone's house onto the desktop. Opening the video, he played it on loop and turned up the volume on the laptop. Taking out the handgun he pulled off Bishop, he wiped away his prints and slid it under the driver seat. He began wiping down the rest of the vehicle and recovered his flash drive. Exiting the vehicle, he locked it and returned to the detective who had stopped puking. "Let me help you to your car, Detective," he said. Bishop nodded his head and allowed Wolf to lead him back to the cruiser.

When they reached the vehicle, the detective turned to Wolf, "Thank you," he said. "Who are you anyway? I feel like I have seen you before or something."

Wolf pulled off his hat, revealing his scarred face. The detective's eyes widened with realization and fear. Bishop reached for his gun, only to find an empty holster. He turned back to face the marred face of the marine when his world faded to black. Wolf had clocked him with a swift elbow to the temple, causing the detective to crumple to the floor. He put his hat back on and unlocked the back door of the detective's car. Hoisting the man into the back seat, he shut the door, locking Bishop inside. "Sleep tight, Detective."

Wolf remembered seeing a payphone in the bar by the front door. He walked inside, picked up the phone with a rag and called 9-1-1. Within three rings someone answered the phone. Without saying a word, Wolf dropped the phone, letting it dangle by the chord, and went back to his Chevelle. Starting the car, he drove out of the parking lot and down the street, parking a good distance away. Within ten minutes, four police cars pulled up. Bishop was awake in the backseat, still vomiting from the Ipecac. Wolf watched as the officers tried to get the car door open. One of them pointed toward the laptop monitor and began asking Bishop questions.

Smiling slightly to himself, Wolf started the Chevelle again. "Hope this helps, Kate," he said, then put the car in gear and headed home.

# Chapter 14

# The Secret Past

June 9th, 2013, 11:30 a.m. Wolf awoke to the sound of his phone buzzing on the nightstand. He picked it up to hear Detective Kate Westbrooke on the other end, "Will, we have Bishop. Some beat cops found him locked in the back of his service car last night blackout drunk, covered in his own vomit. Partner that with a certain video playing on his laptop: he is in a lot of hot water."

"Is that right?" Wolf asked, smiling to himself.

"Yep," she said. "He was brought in for questioning. Still hasn't said anything, though he keeps asking for his lawyer; trying to claim that he has been framed. But if my suspicions are correct, it won't be long before Tyrone finds out that we've taken him into custody."

Wolf stretched with a yawn and then scratched his bald head, "I had the same suspicion. How long do we have?"

The detective sighed, "He most likely already knows, which is why I am pushing for a warrant to search his premises."

Wolf thought for a second, "The garage..."

"What?" she asked.

"Search his garage; he has an SUV stored inside. I am willing to bet that it is the vehicle they used when they killed Darnel. If Tyrone knows you're coming, he is going to move it. There isn't much time," he replied.

"I agree. However, I don't think that Bishop will know where Tyrone keeps his stash or the whole ins and outs of the organization. If we are going to pin him for everything, we will need more."

Wolf thought for a second, "What about Damien?"

"Damien? As in Tyrone's right-hand man?"

"That's the one. He was the one who threatened the pastor and his wife. Maybe the beat cops you stationed out front of their place have seen him sniffing about."

"But how would we make him flip on Tyrone?" the detective asked.

"Kate," Wolf replied, "Use Bishop as leverage on Damien, and Damien as leverage on Bishop. Simple PSYOPS."

"I like the way you think," Kate said, after a moment of pause to think it over. "I will let you know if we find him. And, Will?"

"Yeah?"

"Ever think about being a detective?"

Wolf chuckled, "Let me think about it."

"Better think fast; we could use you here."

"First we get Tyrone, then I plan out my life."

"As long as that plan includes becoming a detective and getting to know a certain pretty little brunette better, I am all for it."

"Goodbye, Kate."

She laughed, "Alright, alright. I will call you when we have more." Wolf thanked her and ended the call. He had been walking through the house during the conversation, now standing in front of the bedroom door he discovered unlocked the night before. All his questions, all the uncertainty of where Darnel was in his mental and emotional health before his passing, was going to be answered behind that door. Wolf took a breath and opened the door, walking inside.

Seeing the room in the daylight, it amazed him how much this room contradicted the one Darnel lived in downstairs. The queen-sized bed was neatly made, and an indent in the pillow on the left showed someone had been sleeping in it recently. There was a pleasant aroma that was warmed by the morning sun pouring through the open blinds; much better than the stale beer smell in the other room. The overall environment was completely different from the cave-like atmosphere he was living in. This one had a certain life to it as well as a woman's touch, evident by the color choice and how they aligned with the decorations around the room. Photos of Darnel and a beautiful blonde woman adorned the walls. Some were cute nature photos, others were obviously wedding pictures: Darnel standing at the front of a church, watching as his bride walked down the aisle; their first kiss as man and wife; and cutting the cake.

Wolf had never seen pictures of Delilah before, but he now understood why when Darnel spoke of her, it was with awe and reverence for who she was. If her character was even a fraction of the beauty of her physical features, then she was truly an amazing woman. Even in these little glimpses of Darnel's memories frozen in time, Wolf could tell that she was something special. Tears began to well up in his eyes, but for the first time in a very long time, the tears were not from grief. Darnel was reunited with the woman he loved; what could be more beautiful than that?

Walking slowly around the room, he took in everything he could. Sitting across from the bed was a small entertainment center with a flat-screen TV hooked up to a DVD player. Finding the remotes, he powered on the television and pressed *play*. After a few moments of buffering, a young blonde woman in a white dress sat in front of the camera: Delilah. She was so radiant, so beautiful. "Hi Darnel," she said with a smile, "Today is October 16th, 2005, and it is only two hours before we get married." She paused as tears began to well up in her eyes. "I am so excited I can barely breathe. To think, I get to spend the rest of my life with you…"

The picture shifted to a video of Darnel standing in front of a crowd in a slick black tuxedo on a stage. He was smiling fondly down the aisle. Wolf instantly recognized the pews and the small sanctuary. It was the church, long before Matt and his wife had taken over as lead pastors. The camera panned over to reveal Delilah standing in the entryway of double doors, in her white dress, standing arm and arm with an elderly man. She began walking down the aisle; everyone stood. Truly a beautiful sight. Wolf watched the wedding in awe as they went on to exchange vows, Darnel kissing the bride, and everyone cheering.

As the footage switched to the reception, Wolf noticed a newspaper sitting next to the television. The front page was of a mangled 1996 Toyota Celica SRS with the headline, *Fatal Crash First Day of Snow*. The date read December 3rd, 2006. "Three months before Darnel enlisted…" Wolf said quietly to himself. He read silently from the paper. *It was late at night; the couple was driving home after the wife had picked up her husband from working swing shift. Investigators believed the car had caught a patch of ice, sending it off the road, slamming into an embankment. The wife was in the passenger seat and had laid her seat all the way back, perhaps in hopes for rest. The husband was behind the wheel when he lost control of the vehicle. The driver side airbag went off, saving the husband. However, the wife was thrown through the windshield. It is unclear whether she was wearing her seatbelt or not. She died from internal hemorrhaging in her husband's arms. She was twenty-one years old. The husband asked to keep their identities confidential.*

Wolf knew that the wife was Delilah. He remembered how much Darnel hated driving in the snow. Whenever anyone asked him why, he would simply say that he had his reasons. It also explained why Darnel joined the Marines when he did and why he blamed himself and God for his wife's death. Wolf began to shake as tears formed in his eyes. So much pain, so much regret.

Next to the newspaper article was a hand-written letter on notebook paper. Wolf wiped his eyes and picked up the piece of parchment. The handwriting was Darnel's; the ink of the pen was still unfaded. He was taken aback by who the letter was addressed to. It wasn't to Delilah, Matt, Jessica, Kate, or even himself. The letter was addressed to God. Wolf took a deep breath and read the letter aloud to himself.

"Dear God," he began, "As I sit here staring at the worst day of my life on paper with the best day of my life on video, I can't help but wonder how I did not see You in all of it. That night Delilah left this world, I so badly wished to leave with her. That is why I joined the Marines and went into active combat, but You kept me safe. Even in the valley of the shadow of death, You protected me. In that, You brought Wolf alongside me when we needed each other the most. I needed someone to look out for and protect and he needed someone to show him what unconditional love from a brother really means. I know that You have plans for my life. Plans not to harm me but give me hope for the future.

"Before I met Matt and Jessica, I never believed that there was any hope for my future, I didn't even believe there was a hope for my day. My life became one of distance, only allowing Wolf and Beef into my own little world. But You redeemed me, You called me out of the valley of dry bones and ransomed me from the ashes. In all of it, You have been by my side and when I called, You answered me. Father, thank You, thank You for never giving up on me. And most importantly, thank You for Delilah and the time I had with her. Though it has been hard without her, I know that she is with You and she is full of joy and wonder of who You are for her. I have never said this before, Father, but... I am sorry for blaming You for her death. With a broken and contrite heart, I have sinned against You by holding this against You.

Today, I lay it at Your feet. Thank You for all that You have done for me. And thank You for my brother Will. I love You, Father. Amen."

Tears flooded down Wolf's cheeks as he laid the letter back on the newspaper article and sat on the bed in silence. This room was a place Darnel hid from for so many years, fighting overseas and then in a bottle when he came back home. But at the end of his life, he had found peace with the loss of his wife and had come back to the church they got married in. Whatever Darnel found in that place, Wolf knew that he wanted to find the same for himself.

# Chapter 15

# The Loved

June 9th, 2013, 12:30 p.m. Wolf's phone rang; it was Jessica. After reading the letter, he had found some home movies of Darnel and Delilah and was watching them. He saw how happy they were and how beautiful they were together. His heart broke for Darnel, yet he found peace that they were now together once more. He wiped the tears from his eyes and cleared his nose before answering the phone. "Good morning. I was beginning to wonder when I would hear from you again," he said.

"Good morning to you too," she said. Her voice was warm and gentle but still showed signs of concern, "I heard you had a crazy night."

Wolf chuckled, "Oh yeah? What part exactly?"

"How about the men breaking into your home?" she said.

"Six less dirty cops off the streets. I would say that's a win."

"You promised to be safe, Will," she said, her voice sounding a little more worried than before.

"I am safe. This will all be over soon, I promise," he assured her.

"I hope so. You sound tired, Will. I didn't wake you, did I?"

Wolf smiled, "Nah, I have been up for a little while now. I am actually in the room upstairs."

"Wait, you mean Darnel and Delilah's room?" she asked.

"That's the one," he replied. "Get this, the door was unlocked."

"Really? Wow!" she replied. "How nice is it? I bet it's really nice."

Wolf stood up and began walking around the room, "It is super clean." He noticed two doors attached to the room that he hadn't checked out just yet. Opening the door to the left, he walked into the adjacent little room, clicking on the light to reveal a walk-in closet. "And apparently it has a walk-in closet."

"Wow, all he is missing is the master bathroom."

Wolf chuckled, "Well, there is another door I haven't checked out yet."

"Well check it out!" she encouraged.

Wolf stepped back out of the walk-in closet and went into the other door to reveal a large bathroom, complete with a standing shower and a large bathtub. "Ding, ding, ding, we have a winner."

"Ha!" Jessica exclaimed, "Does that mean I get to have it? I mean, you did say I won."

Wolf smiled, "I was thinking dinner."

There was a brief pause on the phone; Jessica took in a quick breath, "I think that could suffice. Though it will have to be *some* dinner. I mean, the other option is a master bathroom just for me."

Wolf laughed, "I will see what I can do. What are you doing tonight?"

She sighed and made a groaning sound. "I have to work; my shift starts at 8:30. I still need to finish my laundry and get some sleep. How about breakfast tomorrow morning, say 7?"

"Steak and eggs?" Wolf asked

"Sounds good to me."

"I will see you then. Have a good night at work," he said with a smile and a wink at Beef, who was laying on the floor a few feet away.

"And you get some rest. I want you awake for our first date."

"Yes, ma'am." They said their goodbyes and got off the phone. Wolf walked back into the bedroom and looked at the wedding photos of Darnel and Delilah. "What do you think, Beef?" he asked his little white companion. The dog lifted his head so they were making eye contact. "Think I can have the happiness Darnel had?" Beef let out a *gruff* and wagged his tail excitedly. "I hope you're right," Wolf said. Then he grabbed the duffle bag that he had left in the room the night before, carrying it downstairs and into the garage to put it in the trunk of the Chevelle.

Wolf Jackson

# Chapter 16

# The Reckoning

June 9th, 2013, 5:00 p.m. Wolf had taken a nap and gotten some food in him. He began to be less excited about his date and more concerned about the case. His thoughts went to Damien threatening Matt's wife and kids. The pastor was so angry and scared last night; Wolf hoped he was alright. Just then, his phone rang: it was Kate.

"Hey what's up, Kate?"

"Will, have you heard from the pastor this morning?" Her voice was verging on almost panicked. Something was wrong.

"No, I haven't. Your beat cops afraid to knock on the door?" Wolf asked. "I mean, I get it; I get worried about him preaching at me too."

"Will!" the detective said, the worry evident in her voice. "There wasn't enough evidence to keep the patrol outside the pastor's house; they haven't been there since this morning. Nobody knows what happened exactly, but it doesn't look good."

Wolf sat back for a moment, "What are you saying, Kate?"

She sighed, "They aren't home, and I can't get ahold of the pastor on his cell phone. Can you swing by the church and see if he is there?"

Wolf poured his coffee into a to-go cup and whistled for Beef. "I am already on my way," he said as he went into the garage, back to the Chevelle. He opened the back door so Beef could jump in and grabbed the leather jacket from the back seat, slipping it on. He got behind the wheel, started up the car, and pulled out of the driveway.

He arrived just down the road from the church in twenty minutes. As he neared the parking lot, he saw an SUV parked right in front of the church. Though he could not place it, he knew that vehicle. Being cautious, Wolf passed up the parking lot and rounded back around the block to the back alley behind the church. Throwing the car in park, he pulled the tactical mask out of his pocket and stared at it. Tossing it to the back seat, he grabbed the duffle bag from the trunk, then motioned at Beef with his pinky and thumb pointed towards him. "Stay Beef," he said.

Leaving the car and his best friend behind, he made his way silently to the church, putting the hood of his leather jacket on as he ran. Wolf crouched at the side of the building and peeked around the corner. Two men were at the front door, both packing MP5's. He set the duffle bag on the ground and pulled out his M4 with suppressor already attached, and four mags. He turned off the safety and slid back the bolt to feed the first round into the chamber. He took a quick breath and stood up, firing four rapid shots, two for each man. Both men fell to the ground gripping a knee and a shoulder. Wolf slung the duffle bag behind his back and ran to the front door.

Opening the door with one hand, he slipped into the foyer of the church. He heard a woman scream, "Stop it!" The shout came from the sanctuary. He had to move, *now*.

Bursting through the double doors, into the sanctuary, Wolf quickly assessed his surroundings. He was well aware that all eyes were now on him. Seven men, all armed, turned and trained their guns on him. Matt and his family were on their knees in the middle of the sanctuary. The pastor had blood trickling down from his eyebrow.

There was a man directly to Wolf's left with a shotgun trained on him. Another man stood directly to his right carrying an MP5. Two more men were standing at the front of the church, one on each side of the stage, both carrying small submachine guns. Three men stood in the aisle: the man in the middle was holding an AK-47; the two on the sides were holding shotguns.

"Drop the gun," the man in the middle said. Wolf unclipped the M4 from the shoulder strap and placed it on the ground to his right. "And the duffle bag." Wolf complied and laid it on the ground to his left. "Stand up." Wolf did as he said. "Remove your hood." Wolf slowly rose up his hand and pulled back his hood. All the men grimaced when his face was revealed. Wolf just stared coldly at all of them. "You get that overseas?" the man asked.

Wolf raised his good eyebrow at him but remained silent. "Oh, come on man. It's obvious! Only a trained man could do what you've done the last forty-eight hours and I have to say, I'm impressed. What are you: Marines, Navy, Army, what?"

Wolf just stared at him. The man was beginning to get frustrated. "What's your name?" Still, Wolf remained silent. The man looked to the two men standing beside him. "Take his weapons and gear." He pointed his rifle at Wolf. "Hands behind your head, now!" he spat. Wolf did as he was told.

"I let you take me prisoner, and the holy man and his family go free," Wolf said bluntly. He watched the two men walking towards him closely. They both had their guns trained on him and were about ten feet from him now.

The man in the middle of the room shrugged his shoulders. "I wish I could, but then again, I would love to see your face as you watch them burn," he said with a wicked smile flashing across his face.

Wolf's blood ran cold. "You must be Damien." The man smiled at him. Wolf shrugged his shoulders, "Guess you are as dumb as you look." The smile on the man's face faded away.

"Get him," he said. The men were within arms distance of him now.

"You should have brought more men," Wolf replied. "Down!" Wolf screamed at the pastor and his family as he pulled a flashbang grenade out of his sleeve, throwing it at the assailants before diving behind a pew. Though the pew absorbed most of the blast, Wolf's ears were still ringing and his eyesight was blurred momentarily. Wolf got out from behind the pew and rushed the two gunmen that were still standing there dazed by the grenade. He grabbed the arm of the man on his right and pushed it straight into the air so that the muzzle of the gun was pointed upward. The MP5 went off just over the assailant to the left's head, causing him to dive to the ground. Wolf twisted the gunman's wrist violently, breaking it, forcing him to drop his weapon in agony. He pulled out his pistol with his left hand and shot out the gunman's knees, dropping him to the floor. Wolf drew his knife and spun on his knee, slicing behind the knee of the assailant behind him and fired a round into another assailant's foot. Releasing the knife, he caught the man with the wounded foot right in the jaw with a heavy fist, knocking him out. Wolf then came back with an elbow, catching the man he cut behind the knee in the temple, knocking him unconscious as well.

Shots rang out from the two men by the stage and the man in the middle of the room. Wolf retrieved his M4 and dove into a pew on his right. He aimed over the top of the pew in front of him and fired three shots to the right of the stage where the tip of a muzzle flashed. The sound of a body crashing into the wall and grunts of a man who just got popped in the ballistic vest, told him he had hit his mark. He rolled back through the aisle and behind the pews on the left. He heard bullets ripping into the pews on his right. Wolf popped up and fired three more rapid shots to the left of the stage, only to hear the cracking of wood.

He ducked back down behind the pew and listened. The two gunmen were both firing. Damien was still in the middle; he was too close to the hostages to risk taking out, right at this moment. The shotgun shells from the other man came from his left, about halfway down the aisle. Wolf once again popped up and fired three more rounds to his left. A body crashed to the floor in response, with a shout of pain. Wolf smiled, but now he had a new problem: he was out of ammo and the men seemed to have recovered from the stun grenade. He set the gun silently on the ground and reached into his pocket to pull out a green apple.

Taking a big bite, he dove into the center aisle, tucking his shoulder and rolling forward. He slung the apple as hard as he could down the aisle. He watched it explode on Damien's face, obscuring the man's vision and making him turn away. Wolf sprinted toward Damien. The momentarily blinded assailant began to lift the rifle up like he was going to smack Wolf in between the eyes. Wolf ducked to the right and spat the mushed apple pieces he had in his mouth into the other man's face, making him hesitate. Wolf capitalized, kicking the AK-47 out of Damien's hands. The man retorted by throwing a right cross at Wolf, catching him in the mouth, busting open his lip.

Wolf stumbled back a step, then recovered. Damien was still trying to get the apple juices out of his eyes. Wolf moved swiftly, planting his right foot on a pew and launching himself into the air. He whipped the same foot around as fast as he could and caught the thug in the jaw, sending him flying into the pews on the other side of the aisle. Wolf followed through the kick, spinning in the air and landing with his left foot forward and his right foot behind him, balancing his body. He looked up to see Matt and his family still on their knees a few feet in front of him, with their mouths wide open.

"Shalom," he said with a nod.

Matt, still in shock, responded, "Mazel tov."

Wolf smiled, "Call Detective Westbrooke. Tell her we have Damien and the SUV."

"Shouldn't we call an ambulance instead?" the pastor asked.

"Why? Are you guys hurt?" Wolf asked.

The young pastor raised his eyebrows and motioned towards the men lying on the ground. "Ah," Wolf responded, seeming to have forgotten for a moment about the men he had just dispatched. "I thought you wanted to take them into confession. Your church, Father, do as you wish." Wolf turned, retrieved his weapons and duffle bag, and sprinted back to the Chevelle before Matt could respond. He heard Matt call out a thank you behind him as he ran.

Beef greeted him with a *gruff* and he scratched the little, fat beast's head. He pulled out his phone and called Jessica; the phone rang a few times. "Pick up... c'mon pick up the phone," he said, tapping his foot on the floor of the Chevelle. Her voice sounded through the speaker.

"Hi this is Jess; I can't come to the phone right now. If you need to contact me, you can try my work cell at 303-562-1136. Feel free to leave me a message after the beep." An annoying beep sounded through the speaker.

"Jess, it's Will, I'm going to try your other phone. Tyrone's men just tried to kill Matt and his family. It's too close to the attack from those dirty cops last night. This is all going haywire. I need to know where you are. Call me when you get this," Wolf said into the phone. He hung it up and punched in the other number, then listened as it rang.

Jessica's frantic voice rang out, "Hello?"

"Jess? I thought you were going to work in a couple hours?" he asked, trying to keep his voice calm.

"Will?" she responded. "Yeah sorry, I got called in early. We are swamped. I have three people in my ER that are critical. I have to go; but don't worry, we are still on for breakfast."

"Jess, there was—" he began to say, before beeping sounds and people shouting started going off in the background.

"Oh man," came Jessica's frantic voice, "Will, I have to go. See you soon." And with that, she hung up the phone.

Just then, Detective Kate Westbrooke pulled into the church parking lot with two patrol cars. Wolf got out of the Chevelle and flagged them down. Kate exited her vehicle. "Will, what happened?"

Wolf pointed his thumb behind himself to the church, "Damien and four goons tried to torch the pastor and his family alive. I came by to check on the pastor and had to make contact."

Kate nodded, "Anyone dead?"

Wolf shook his head, "No ma'am. But there is the SUV I think you have been looking for," he said, motioning to the vehicle parked in the parking lot.

She nodded and signaled for the beat cops to go inside. Once they were alone, she turned to Wolf, "Will, you were in two gunfights in less than 24 hours. That doesn't look good. We may need to put you into witness protection."

Wolf shook his head, "Negative. We have Damien. Make him flip on Tyrone by making him think Bishop flipped on him. It will be fine."

She sighed, "Will, you don't understand. With Bishop arrested I am now the highest-ranking officer. I can't have a civilian chasing people down with guns out here."

"You sent me here, remember?" he asked.

"Yes," she responded, "though I did not think you would get in another firefight. I can't be held responsible for your name in the database. People will start thinking that you are a vigilante."

Wolf thought for a second, "Deputize me or hire me as some sort of consultant."

She shook her head, "That won't exonerate you from killing someone, Will."

Raising his hands straight out in exasperation, Wolf stared at her for a moment. "Name one person I have killed in the last week. One. You can't, because I don't kill."

"That's not the point, Will," she retorted.

"What is the point then?" Wolf asked, the frustration eminent in his voice.

She paused and took in a deep breath, "Tyrone is gone, Will. We can't find him. We went to his house with the search warrant and he wasn't there. No one knows where he is, but we are sure he is coming after you. Please, let me protect you."

Lowering his hands, Wolf realized the gravity of Kate's words. He nodded his head, "Alright, alright. What happens now?"

She let out a sigh of relief, "Well, we have to take these guys into custody; don't have room in the cars for you too. Start an investigation here and see what we can figure out about the attack. Could you meet us at the station to get you squared away?"

He nodded, "Let me talk to the holy man for a minute." Kate agreed just as one of the two cops came out with Damien in cuffs.

"Is this the one you want, ma'am?" the officer asked.

Kate nodded, "Yes, thank you. How are the others?"

"Two need an ambulance." The officer gestured towards Wolf, "Your friend here can handle himself." Then he reached his hand out to Wolf who took it and shook it firmly, "Well done, sir."

"My pleasure," Wolf responded.

Kate told the officer to put all the men in a contained area until the paramedics arrive and to tape off the area. "This is now a crime scene and that SUV is a huge part of it. Do not leave this man alone," she said as she loaded Damien into the back of her car. The cop walked over to his cruiser and began taping off the area.

Wolf and Kate walked into the church and met the pastor and his wife. "Hey," the pastor said, "what's happening?"

Wolf motioned to the young female detective, "This is Detective Kate Westbrooke. She will be asking your wife some questions while you and I talk." Matt nodded and both of them went to the corner of the sanctuary.

"So, what's going on?" the pastor asked.

"Tyrone is missing; they want me in witness protection. But I think I know where he is going, and if I am right, I can't stay here any longer. I have a small window while they are distracted."

Matt nodded, "What do you need me to do?"

Wolf smiled. "Stop saying nice things. You're making me start to like you, Father," he said, and they both chuckled. Then Wolf got serious, "If I am right, I might not make it back. Beef is going to need a good home..." he said.

Matt looked to the ground for a moment and nodded his head, "We will take care of him until you come back." He then put his hand on Wolf's shoulder, "But make no mistake, brother, you are coming back."

Wolf nodded and then they both slipped out of the church and walked over to the Chevelle. Opening the trunk, Wolf pulled out a leash and went to the front door to let Beef out. Hooking the leash to his collar, he got down on one knee so that he and his best friend were eye to eye. "I have to go Beef. I might not come back." The dog moaned slightly. "I know buddy, I know. But I need you to be strong and watch after the pastor and his family for me. They are good people. Can you do that?" Beef licked Wolf's chin. "Good boy," Wolf said, and scratched him on the head. He stood up and handed the leash to Matt.

The pastor took it and then embraced Wolf. Out of reaction, Wolf felt himself wanting to wrench out of the hug, but instead, he found himself embracing the pastor back. "Father God," the pastor began, "I stand before you with my brother, Will. You placed in this man a warrior's heart, and a tenacity to do what is right, even in the midst of great opposition. I pray that You walk with him tonight and that Your hand protects him as he storms the gates of hell. May You be the source of his strength as our strength comes from You and You alone. For as it says in Your Word, even in the valley You are with us.

Therefore, we do not need to fear evil because You protect us. May You bless Will as You once blessed David and his mighty men. Thank You for Will, I trust that You will return him to us as the man You have called him to be. In faith and Your Holy Name, we pray. Amen."

"Amen," Wolf repeated. He stepped back from the pastor and looked down at Beef. "Stay boy," he said, then jumped into his car. He started it up and drove past the police officer, leaving the church parking lot before anyone could follow.

# Chapter 17

# The Wolf

June 9th, 2013, 7:30 p.m. Wolf pulled into the parking garage of the hospital. Driving slowly, he searched for any of the vehicles he had seen at Tyrone's house. On the fifth floor of the parking garage, he saw the Camaro, Jeep, and Hummer parked next to two *SWAT* cars. Parking across from them, he noticed the license plates of the *SWAT* vehicles.

Taking out his phone, he took pictures and sent them to Kate Westbrooke, saying, "Look what I found at the hospital." His phone instantly started ringing. He answered it.

"Will, you need to get out of there," Kate said, as soon he picked up.

"Who are the SWAT guys?"

"Bishop flipped on them; they work for Tyrone."

"How many?"

"If they are all there: six, not counting Tyrone's goons. Let the police handle this, Will."

"Negative. Jess is working tonight. I am not taking chances."

"Will, if you go in there, I have to arrest you." Her voice was assertive.

"See you soon, Detective," he said, then hung up the phone.

Reaching into the back seat, he pulled out his shotgun, set it on his lap and began loading it. Pulling a shoulder belt loaded with shotgun shells out of the bag, he removed his jacket and attached the belt around his right shoulder at an angle so that it wrapped around his chest and strapped under his left armpit. There was a carabiner on the left side of the belt next to his ribcage. He hooked his shotgun onto it, so the butt of the gun was behind his left shoulder and the barrel ended right before his waist. Once it was secured, he put his jacket back on. He reached behind the seat, grabbed his M4, and strapped it to his right shoulder, letting it hang by his right ribcage. He stuffed six mags for his M4 into the inside pockets of his jacket.

He grabbed his M&P .45 from the front seat and put it in the back of his pants, hiding it under his shirt. He stuffed five mags into his pants pockets, taking a quick breath to solidify his nerves, and got out of the car. Wolf walked over to the elevator with his M4 in rest position and hit the button. The doors opened and he entered the elevator, selecting the main floor, and rode the car down.

Some people's eyes widened when he came walking in with the gun. A male staff went to intercept him. "Are you with the cops?" the man asked.

Wolf nodded, "Where they posted?"

"They are in the ER, sir. They have closed it off. Said there was a threat," the man replied.

Wolf took in what the man was saying, "I need you to call the cops and tell them everything that they told you. Leave nothing out."

The man looked at him with some confusion, "Um, okay?"

"Good. Now where is the ER?" he asked. The man pointed down the hall to the right.

"Follow the signs," he said.

Wolf nodded his thanks. Then, keeping his gun at the ready, he began jogging down the hallways, searching for Tyrone and his men. His pace was swift and steady, pausing only when he had to round corners. His arm ached from his previous wound, making it difficult to keep his rifle raised. Correcting his mind, he blocked out the pain, focusing on the task at hand. He rounded a corner to find two men armed with submachine guns and body armor, walking down the hallway in front of him.

One man spotted him and started to raise his weapon. Wolf fired first, catching the man in the stomach, causing him to stumble backwards. His partner turned and hip-fired at Wolf, narrowly missing him as he lunged back around the corner. The man he had shot in the stomach seemed to recover enough to join his buddy. Both machine guns blared as bullets tore at the wall, breaking it piece by piece.

Wolf searched the area, pinned down in his current position; he needed a new plan of attack. Across the hall, about fifteen feet from him, was a room; the door was closed, but it would have to do. He just needed an opening. Suddenly the gunfire went silent as magazines were being slid from both guns to reload. Wolf capitalized. With a quick three step, he dropped into a baseball slide across the polished tile floor. He fired his weapon in controlled spurts down the hallway, causing the other two men to fumble with reloading their weapons. His body slammed into the closed door and he pressed himself against it as bullets from his enemies once again began to fill the small space.

Wolf tried to jiggle the handle with his left hand while firing the rifle with his right. The door was locked. He smacked the door with his hand as bullets skimmed by his body, narrowly missing him. His mag had run out; he let the M4 fall underneath his right arm as he threw back his jacket, pulling his shotgun from its hook. He tumble-rolled into the center of the hallway and fired his shotgun. One of the men flew backwards as the round caught him in the chest piece of his body armor.

The other man dove into a room on his left and put his weapon out the door, blindly unloading the entire magazine in an amateur effort to take down his assailant. Rolling out of the line of fire, Wolf racked another round into the chamber of his Remington Tactical and fired at the door frame, catching the submachine gun, shattering the front half of the small weapon. The man dropped it and disappeared into the room. He re-emerged with a pistol and began to pop off shots at Wolf.

A burning sensation ripped into Wolf's left shoulder as he tried to drop to the ground to evade the blind shots. Releasing his shotgun, Wolf grabbed his knife and put it under his jacket near his injured left shoulder. The man emerged from the room, his pistol aimed at Wolf's head. "Stay down," the gunman said.

Wolf lay there motionless. The man stepped closer to him until he was standing near his right hip, his firearm still trained on Wolf's head. In a quick motion, the knife snapped out from under the jacket and sliced into the gunman's right achilles tendon. The man let out a loud scream and dropped to the ground. Wolf lunged forward and drove his right elbow into the man's jaw, rendering him unconscious. He pulled out his knife and wiped it on the unconscious man's shirt.

Staggering to his feet, Wolf retrieved his shotgun, clipping it back to his chest belt, letting it hang once more. His shoulder bled under his jacket, causing it to stick to his shirt. He mentally forced his body to block the pain out as best as he could. Changing out the mags in his M4, he began walking down the hallway, towards the ER once more. His gait was a little slower than before, a little more cautious. His heart raced with adrenaline, making his blood pump faster and increasing his blood loss; he needed to find Jessica, fast.

Wolf heard a door open behind him; he ducked just in time as a bullet buried itself into the wall in front of him. He dove to his right, driving a shoulder into the door next to him, bursting it open, causing him to fall onto the floor within. Spinning to a seated position, he trained his assault rifle at the door. A canister landed at his feet, releasing smoke rapidly into the small room. Wolf rolled behind the bed as the room began to disappear before his eyes. Above his head was an oxygen mask that was made to cover the whole face. He grabbed the mask and slid it on before he breathed in any of the gas. Bullets cracked into the floor and wall close to where he had landed. His eyes were burning; tears began to form, making it hard to see. From the sound of the shots, Wolf counted three burst shot weapons firing into the room. Pulling out his empty M4 mag, Wolf chucked it to the other side of the room where a crash rang out.

The clatter of boots entered the room as bullets ripped into the wall close to where he had thrown his mag. Wolf aimed his rifle at the center of the room and began popping off controlled bursts, about knee height. He heard a body crash to the floor as a man let out a scream. Wolf launched himself across the bed, rolling off his back, and landed on one knee as bullets drilled into the wall on the other side of the bed. Wolf fired at the flashes from the muzzles of the guns. Two more bodies crashed to the floor and Wolf felt his way out of the room. His eyes were watering uncontrollably, and he was coughing violently.

Wolf bent over, putting his hands on his knees in the hallway, trying to clear his eyes and lungs. Something cold pressed on the back of his neck. "Drop the rifle and the shotgun. Remove the jacket," a man's voice said. Wolf slowly unhooked the M4 from its sling and set it on the tile floor, followed by the shotgun. Removing his jacket, he set it on the ground as well, raising his hands and slowly stood up. "Do you have any other weapons on you?" the man asked.

Wolf nodded his head; his eyes began to clear up. "The knife in my boot and the pistol in the small of my back."

The man removed the weapons, keeping them on his person. "Put your hands behind your back," he said, as he stepped in front of Wolf. He had a pump-action shotgun trained on Wolf's chest.

"I can't," Wolf said.

The man looked at Wolf's bleeding shoulder and bicep and smiled, "Fine, arms in front then." Wolf obeyed the order and the man zip-tied his hands together. He gave Wolf a rough push. "Walk."

Wolf did as he was told, walking in front of the man. His eyes continued to clear up as they walked down the hallway. They paused in front of a pair of elevator doors and the man hit the button. After a few moments, the doors opened to reveal a large elevator.

"Get in," the gunman said. Wolf complied and stepped inside. The man kept his shotgun trained on him as he stepped in and pressed the button. Floor number six. There was a pause as the doors closed and the car began to rise.

Wolf looked over at his captor. He was different from the rest: he wasn't wearing body armor. Instead, he wore a royal blue dress shirt, tucked into his pants, revealing a detective badge hanging from his belt. "Where are you taking me?" Wolf asked.

The man smirked, "Aspect has something special planned for you."

Wolf looked away to assess his own injuries. His shoulder and bicep were both still trickling blood. He glanced up at the digital screen that told them what floor they were on. They were on floor number five: he would be on floor six soon. He staggered on his feet and rested his right shoulder on the wall of the elevator, acting as if the blood loss had taken its toll on his body.

The doors opened and his captor motioned with his shotgun, "Let's move." Wolf stayed exactly where he was. "I said, walk!" the man ordered, as he stepped in front of him to put his gun up against Wolf's head.

In a quick motion, Wolf pushed the barrel of the gun up and ducked so that when the gun went off, it blasted a hole in the wall instead of his head. He grabbed the foregrip of the gun and twisted it up against the wall on his right side. The man tried to rip the gun from Wolf's hands, but he held firm. He drove his left elbow into the man's sternum, knocking the wind from his lungs. Wolf kicked the buttons on the door, hitting a few different numbers. The doors closed and the elevator car began to move again.

The corrupt detective kicked Wolf on the inseam of his left leg; Wolf countered with a left elbow to the face. Releasing the shotgun with his left hand, the detective punched Wolf in his wounded shoulder repeatedly. Wolf cried out but held firm to the weapon.

The man tried to punch him in the shoulder again, but Wolf twisted his body, yanking both men off the wall and onto the floor. Wolf landed on top of his attacker, still holding onto the foregrip of the shotgun. Another shot rang out, denting the elevator doors next to the two men. The attacker drove his right knee into Wolf's ribcage and twisted his body, reversing position so that Wolf was on his back. His shoulder screamed in pain as the man pressed the shotgun down on his chest and then tried to yank it free from his grasp.

Wolf knew that his opponent had the upper hand. His injury was taking its toll: he was losing blood fast. His opponent yanked violently on the shotgun again and then dropped down to push it onto Wolf's chest once more. This time Wolf pulled the shotgun to him and launched his head off the tile floor, catching his attacker on the bridge of the nose with his forehead. Blood sprayed from the man's nose like a fire hydrant as he lurched back in pain.

Wolf yanked down on the shotgun, causing the man to jerk forward. Planting his feet onto the man's hips, he exploded with his leg muscles, launching the bloody attacker into the wall behind him. The elevator shook at the violent slam of the man's body as he crumpled to the ground in a heap. Jumping to his feet, Wolf turned towards the momentarily stunned man and drove his right boot into the man's face, sending a spray of blood across the wall and knocking him out instantly.

Wolf dropped to his knees next to the man and began to search his body. He retrieved his knife from the man's jacket and cut the zip-tie free from his hands, narrowly escaping cutting himself in the process. He sheathed his knife and searched the unconscious detective again, retrieving his pistol and stuffing it in the back of his pants. Sitting the unconscious man up, he zip-tied his hands to the handrail. Wolf pat the man's head and hit the button for floor number seven: the surgical wing.

# Chapter 18

# The Collide

Wolf drew out his pistol and turned the safety off, sliding the rail back slightly to check the chamber: a round was loaded in it. He stepped to the side of the doors and waited for them to open. The elevator stopped moving as it hit its destination. There was a *ding* as the elevator doors slid open, revealing an empty hallway. He stepped out of the elevator and scanned his surroundings. He didn't see any of Tyrone's clowns anywhere, but he still treaded lightly into the hallway. His steps were calculated, swift, smooth, and silent. He took every corner with caution; he couldn't afford to be blindsided again.

Stalking down the hallway like a ghost, Wolf saw a room labeled *ICU*. Checking down the hallway in all directions, he made sure the coast was clear and slipped into the room, silently shutting the door behind him. He flicked on the light to reveal a large room with a bunch of empty beds. Curtains separated the beds from each other. There was a large window showing a smaller room to his right and a door leading into it. Wolf walked over to it, keeping low to the floor. Once inside the room, he saw a cabinet with glass doors being lit up by interior light, revealing the medicine inside.

He broke the lock with the handle of his pistol and opened it up. Inside, he found clotting salts, sanitizing alcohol, burn cream, gauze, and tape. On the counter to the left of the cabinet was a hot plate with a glass beaker on top. Wolf removed the glass beaker; setting it on the counter, he plugged in the hot plate and set the blade of his knife on it. He grabbed the clotting salts, sanitizing alcohol, burn cream, gauze, and tape and set them on the counter next to a sink and a stool. Setting his pistol on the counter to his right, he took his shirt off. Taking some paper towels from the bin, he wiped up the blood from his shoulder, trying to get as much of it cleaned up as possible.

Wolf opened the sanitizing alcohol and poured it into the wound. He grunted slightly, trying to stifle his pain as the clear liquid entered the tender flesh. Setting the bottle back on the counter, he wiped away the excess liquid and ripped open the clotting salts. Taking a deep breath, he poured the salts into the wound. His breath was snatched from his lungs as the pain shot throughout his body. He forced himself to breathe as much as he could. Wolf took a few deep breaths, reached for his shirt and shoved part of it in his mouth. He grabbed the glowing, red-hot knife from the hot plate; his heart raced; his breath became more rapid. Closing his eyes tightly, Wolf put the knife over his wound. Tears formed in his eyes. Burned flesh flooded his nostrils. He let out a muffled scream of agony and then took the knife away from his body, throwing it into the sink.

Wolf spat out his shirt and ripped open the burn cream with his teeth, before applying it to his shoulder. The cream helped subside the pain. He grabbed the sterile gauze, placing it on his shoulder. Grabbing the tape with his right hand, he pulled off a piece, ripping it with his teeth. He set eight strips of tape on the counter and secured the gauze on his wounds. He turned so that he could see his back in the mirror. The shot he had taken in the shoulder was a clean through and through; no bullet to dig out made life easier.

Wolf retrieved his knife and set it back on the hot plate. He let out a deep sigh as it began to glow hot once again. He grabbed the alcohol and began the process he had performed on his shoulder on his back. After another agonizing session, Wolf had successfully sealed the wound. He grabbed his shirt and put it back on, grimacing as he raised his arm over his shoulder. Once he had his shirt back on, he retrieved his pistol and started to head out of the room. There was a sound from the hallway; Wolf cut the lights in the small room he was in and ducked down low.

The door from the hallway opened, causing light to flood into the large room with beds. A man with an assault rifle stepped in slowly, overshadowing the light from the doorway; he crouched low and scanned the room very closely. Just by looking at him, Wolf could tell that this man was ex-military, more than likely mercenary. He was taller than Wolf, about six foot four inches. His steps were calculated and silent. He was wearing a black Kevlar vest with a t-shirt underneath. His biceps rippled as he held up his assault rifle. It looked to be an AR-15, but in the dark room, Wolf couldn't be sure.

Wolf was outgunned and his right arm was rendered useless. If he had any opportunity to win, he had to act now. Tumble-rolling from his hiding place, Wolf fired three shots at the man. Two of the bullets tore into the drywall, but the third found its home, drilling into the man's bicep. Most of Tyrone's men would have fallen back or hesitated for a long moment due to this, but this seasoned warrior twisted at the pain and unloaded half a mag in Wolf's direction. Wolf dove back into the smaller room and crouched behind the wall for protection.

He heard a chuckle. "They said you were dangerous!" the man exclaimed. His voice was thick with an English accent. "Where'd you do your training?"

"United States Marine Corps," Wolf replied, "What about you?"

"French Foreign Legion," the man replied. "I heard you devil dogs were supposed to be tough, but you take that to a whole new level. I'm willing to wager you were more than just the standard marine."

Wolf let out a chuckle, "Tell you what, throw down that rifle and I will tell you everything."

The man laughed, "Not a chance."

Wolf smiled to himself, "Worth a shot. So, how does a French Foreign Legion get tied up with a drug dealer?"

"Let's just say he pays better than my government."

"Health benefits and everything?" Wolf asked. Before the man could answer, he twisted out of the doorway and fired three more shots. All of them hit their mark: right above the trigger of the AR-15, drilling deep holes into it, rendering it unable to fire. The man let the assault rifle drop as he pulled out his pistol and fired at Wolf. The bullets grazed past Wolf, narrowly missing him.

"Mother Theresa!" the man exclaimed, "That was my favorite gun!"

"Put it on your boss' tab, mate."

The other man chuckled, shaking his head. "Let's do this like men, shall we?" he said, setting his pistol onto the floor. Wolf stood up and looked at him through the doorway. The man spread out his arms and stared at Wolf quizzically, "Still got a bite, devil dog, or are you all bark with a mean look?"

Wolf set his pistol on the counter to his right. He looked at the other man and raised his good eyebrow. Stepping into the larger room, Wolf motioned for the other man to come at him. His assailant smiled and charged him; Wolf did the same. The man launched himself into the air, off his left leg, and cocked his right fist back, aiming to drop a superman punch on Wolf's face. His effort was countered when Wolf dipped his knees, ducking the punch, and caught the man in the chest with his shoulder, expelling the oxygen from the other man's lungs.

Both men went to the ground with Wolf pulled into the guard of his combatant. Wolf began to work his jiu-jitsu, trying to counter the other man's rubber guard so he could deal more damage. The man got his boots into the crook of Wolf's hip bones and launched him off. Wolf crashed into the small room, shattering the glass cabinet. His combatant placed his hands behind his head and rocked back onto them, then sprang up, landing perfectly on his feet. "That all you got, mate?" he said, flashing a wicked grin.

Wolf stood up as well, reached to his right forearm and pulled out a large shard of glass. He looked at it briefly and chucked it to the side, causing it to shatter on the wall. Wolf rose up his hands and motioned for the man to come towards him once more, allowing a devilish smile to cross his scarred face. The Englishman charged like a bull. Wolf blocked a right elbow and countered with a left hook to the body. He was rewarded with a forearm to his face.

Wolf danced away from the cabinet, evading a couple strikes from his assailant. He got around him and slipped through the doors of the small room, back into the larger room; changing the fight from the close quarters match, into a kickboxing match. Slipping a jab, he gave the man a firm leg kick with his right boot, just above the knee. The man's leg buckled. Wolf capitalized with a stiff right cross to the nose of his opponent, causing him to fall onto one of the beds. Blood spurted from the man's nostrils onto the sheets; he smiled, wiped the blood with the loose linens, and got back to his feet. "Nice right hand, mate. Very nice," he said. Wolf could see that he was favoring his left leg as he stood.

Wolf nodded his head, welcoming the other man to come at him once more. His opponent was more hesitant this time; the blood gushing from his nose seemed to make him realize that Wolf was no pushover. He began to throw slight jabs, seeming to gage his reach, trying to put together his rhythm. Wolf played along, avoiding the shots, causing his opponent to reach further and further with each jab he threw.

Once the man felt comfortable, he lunged forward, catching Wolf with a left jab followed by a right hook to the body and a straight left toward his chin. Wolf saw it coming, absorbing the right to the body and slipping the straight left. He threw a combination of his own with a left hook to the exposed rib cage, just six inches below the armpit; he felt two of them crack on impact. Wolf followed up with a violent leg kick, digging his right shin into his opponent's left knee, dislocating it. He thrust his right elbow up into the man's sternum and wrenched his fist straight up, catching the man in the face with his knuckles, causing the Englishman to stumble backwards. He caught him again in the right temple with a spinning back elbow. Collapsing to the floor in a heap, the Englishman fought to get back to his feet. "Stay down," Wolf said sternly.

The Englishman spun and caught Wolf in a scissor leg takedown, forcing him to the ground. He struck his head on the footboard of one of the hospital beds on the way down, causing his head to spin. He felt the other man trying to pass his guard and get him into a full mount. Reacting by pure instinct, Wolf hooked the man's leg with his right arm, and spun, reversing the position. His head started to clear as he felt the other man's legs wrap his neck into a triangle choke.

"That's the thing about us Foreign Legion boys, mate, we don't believe in the term, 'Surrender.' You'll have to do better than that," he mocked, as he squeezed tighter around Wolf's neck.

Wolf could feel his heart beat in his good ear; he was losing oxygen to his brain and would pass out soon. Grabbing onto the other man's forearm with both hands, Wolf used every bit of power he had left in his body to explode into a standing position, gripping firmly to his adversary, ripping him from the floor. Wolf stood straight up, the Englishman over his head, still holding tightly to the choke he had on Wolf as he stared at the severely scarred man in disbelief. In a swift motion, Wolf slammed him onto the tile floor, making his body go limp, releasing Wolf from the chokehold. Wolf dropped a huge right hand onto the Englishman's jaw, ensuring that he would not be getting up anytime soon.

He got up and leaned on one of the beds. He looked at the unconscious man on the floor and let out a chuckle. "Good fight mate, better luck next time," he said. Then he scooped up the other man, with a strained grunt, and placed him onto one of the beds. He pulled out the restraints and strapped the unconscious man down to the bed. Grabbing the I.V., he stuck it into the man's exposed forearm and raised the head of the bed with the remote so that the blood wouldn't clot in his nose and cause him to suffocate.

Walking into the smaller room, he grabbed a needle and a bottle of morphine from the broken cabinet and filled up a syringe. Recovering his pistol from the countertop and stuffing it into the back of his waistband, he walked back to the bedside of the Englishman and screwed the syringe into the I.V., injecting it into the clear liquid. "This should help with your pain, soldier," he said.

Wolf reached into his pocket and pulled out a green apple, taking a big bite out of it while he walked out of the room and into the hallway. He drew out his pistol with his left hand, keeping the apple in his right. He heard a door shut behind him and took another big bite out of his apple, making a loud smack as he ripped a big crispy chunk from the core. Another sound broke the silence of the still hallway: the all too familiar sound of a shotgun pumping another round into the chamber.

"Don't move," a voice said, "Turn around, slowly."

Wolf complied. Keeping his gun hidden, he turned to see a young black teen, he had to be no more than seventeen. He was wearing a beanie, baggie jeans, and an oversized t-shirt, awkwardly holding a shotgun to Wolf's chest. Wolf took another bite from his apple and stared at the kid. After a long pause of silence, Wolf let out a sigh, "What do you think you're doing?"

The kid shifted his feet slightly, trying to keep a tough composure. "Taking you to Aspect," he said uneasily.

Wolf cocked his head slightly, "What's your name, kid?"

"Why do you want to know that?" the kid challenged.

"I just want to know who my arresting officer is."

The kid shifted his feet. "Jace."

Wolf nodded his head. "Jace. That's a nice name. My name is Will," he said smiling. "So, Jace... what if I uh, don't want to go see 'Aspect,' as you call him?"

The kid firmed his grip on the shotgun and gulped hard. He shifted his feet once more. "Then I'll... I'll blow a hole through your chest..." he said, stammering through his sentence.

Wolf nodded his head again and shifted the apple around in his hand. "Trust me, Jace, you don't want to do that."

The kid shifted his feet again. "Don't act like you know me!"

"Oh, I'm not. I just know a frightened man when I see one. You've probably never even shot an animal, let alone a man before. Am I right?" he asked. The kid shifted his feet once more. Wolf nodded his head. "I, on the other hand, have killed many men in my time. I wouldn't hesitate if I were you," he said. He could tell that the kid was trying to figure him out. Wolf, sensing the hesitation, threw his apple into the air towards the kid and yanked his pistol out from behind himself. He shot the apple, causing it to splatter all over the young kid.

At the sound of the gunshot, Jace dropped his shotgun to the ground. Wolf trained his pistol at the kid's head. The frightened kid wiped the apple juice from his eyes and then raised his hands up once he saw Wolf aiming his gun at him. "Don't kill me, man. Please."

Wolf kept the gun trained on him. "I'm not going to kill you, Jace," Wolf said. The kid let out a deep sigh of relief. "But," Wolf continued, Jace's eyes widening once more, "only if you make a deal with me right here. Walk away from this life, go to school, and be somebody worth respecting."

"I don't know how to do that, man!" the kid said abruptly.

"Let me reiterate," Wolf said, "if you don't change your way of living, then I will have to revoke the deal. I'm very well trained, Jace. Believe me, I will find you."

Jace shifted his feet. "Ai'ght man..." he responded.

Wolf nodded his head and put his pistol in the back of his waistband. "Drop any weapons, drugs, your phone, anything that connects you to this life, on the floor and leave it all behind. The cops will be here soon. Get out before they catch you. They won't be as merciful as I am. Do you understand?"

Jace nodded his head and began to do as he was told, setting the paraphernalia on the floor. He started to walk away from Wolf, then turned back towards him. "He's got your girl, man. They're in the ER; there's a stairway two doors down and to the right that they aren't covering. That was my post, but I left it when I heard a crash." He stared at Wolf. "There's four men with him, all carrying SMG's. All are killers."

Wolf nodded. "Thank you, Jace. Now go."

Jace nodded his head in return, "Just repaying the favor..." Then he turned and ran down the hallway. Wolf scooped up the shotgun and checked all the ammo he had on him; he had twelve shells for the shotgun and two and a half clips for his pistol left. It would have to do.

# Chapter 19

# The Justified

Wolf walked to the door that Jace had told him too, opened it silently, and crept into the stairwell. Moving with stealth, he made his way down the stairwell and to the floor below. There was a metal door with a small square window leading to the landing. He peeked through the tiny window and scanned the room. There was movement to the right. His heart sank as he saw four men surrounding a female. Another man, in suit pants and a dress shirt, stood behind her with a 9mm trained on her head. He was barking out orders to the other men, motioning to different positions. Wolf didn't care about him as much as the woman he had in his custody. Wolf could barely breathe; his lungs felt like lead balloons sinking into the pit of his stomach. His arms felt heavy. It took all he had not to scream in rage. His throat finally allowed a hoarse statement to pass his lips. "Jessica…" he said.

He couldn't go flying in there and take them all out while firing from cover. He couldn't risk her life. He surveyed his surroundings: the stairwell was small and made of brick, making it difficult for anyone outside to gage what floor a person would be on by sound alone. Above his head were some metal rails that seemed to give extra support to the landing above. They were about ten feet up.

Taking in a deep breath, he cocked the shotgun and fired a shot over the rail, followed by three more. He released the shotgun, letting it fall to the floors below. He jumped up, grasped the metal bars above his head, and pulled himself up into a parallel position with the landing above. The door crashed open below him and two men came rushing into the small area. Unable to hold his body up any longer, Wolf released the metal rails and let his body land on the two men. He kicked one in the face, causing him to fall back and crack his head on the wall, rendering him unconscious.

The man he landed on began firing off his weapon, causing a dust cloud as bullets ripped into the concrete brick. Wolf wrestled it from his hand and let the weapon fall down the stairs. The man pulled out a spring-loaded pocket knife and tried to stab Wolf in the neck; instead, the blade met the flesh of Wolf's left forearm. Taking his right elbow around, Wolf drove it deep into the man's temple. Wolf pulled the blade from his arm, wiped it off, and then collapsed it down and put it into his pocket. He stood up and was struck in the face by something hard. There was another blow to his midsection, around his kidney, that made him drop to one knee. He took out his combat knife and stabbed his attacker in the knee and then drove his elbow up into the man's chin, knocking him out cold. Another attacker kicked him in the face.

He fell to his back, only remaining conscious by feeling a foot stomp on him repeatedly. He caught the leg and twisted it, dislocating the knee, and drove his boot into the man's inseam. His attacker crashed to the floor right next to him, screaming. Wolf drove his elbow into the man's jaw, silencing the man's screams temporarily. Wolf slowly rose to his feet, his vision blurry. He reached behind his back and pulled out his pistol, turning the safety off. He stumbled to the door, pulled it open, and stepped inside. His vision was still affected, making it difficult for him to tell where he needed to go. Something hot tore into his right shoulder as a gunshot rang out. Wolf crashed into a wall for support, the pain causing his vision to clear.

He looked up to see a man in a sharp pinstripe suit walking toward him. Wolf recognized him as the man he had come here to take down: Tyrone. He tried to raise his pistol to shoot the drug dealer. Before he could get on target, another shot rang out, catching him just above his left knee. Wolf fell to a kneeling position on the floor; he tried to aim his gun once more but was shot again, this time in the chest. Three more shots rang out, all hitting him center mass. Wolf couldn't move; sound faded in and out as his mind fought to remain conscious. He saw Jess on her knees, about twenty feet back from his attacker; she was screaming and crying. His hearing began to come back into focus as his mind finally overcame the pain.

A cynical, demeaning voice filled his good ear. "You really thought you could take me down?" it said, followed by a laugh.

Jessica's voice cried out, "Will, please!"

"Shut up!" the man's voice screamed. He kicked Wolf's pistol away. "Now you did some fine work, my man: sending that car into my gate; taking out my men; leaving your love notes. Talk about psychological warfare." Tyrone paused and shook his head.

"Then you find out Bishop is on my payroll and you take him out too. You're good, you are definitely good. However, I am curious, what was the end game? Huh? What was the point of all of this? Were you just protecting the church, or was it something else? I mean, what would drive a man to go to such an extent?"

He paused for a moment. "Well," he said, "I guess we'll never know." He pointed his gun at Wolf's head, but before it went off, his arm was shoved into the air. Wolf snapped his eyes open and saw Tyrone push Jess off him and strike her with the back of his hand, sending her crashing to the floor. Wolf reached into his pocket, pulled out the pocket knife and flicked it open. Taking every ounce of strength he had in his body, he exploded off the ground, launching himself at Tyrone, and drove the knife into the man's left pectoral. He was rewarded with a violent pistol whip to his face, followed by a rough kick to his chest that sent him sprawling onto his back, sliding across the floor in his own pool of blood.

His world went dark. Sound began to fade into an ominous white noise, and he could only taste the metallic twinge of his own blood pouring into his mouth. He couldn't move. His body was falling into a deep void that he began to embrace, finally feeling the rest he so desired. He could feel peace for the first time in his life. No more fighting, no more nightmares, no more being alone, just peace.

A voice shattered the stillness, "Get on your feet, Marine." It was a soft yet assertive voice. He tried to ignore it, but it broke through the silence once more, this time much more forceful. "I said: get on your feet, Marine!"

His lethargic mind recognized the voice. "Darnel?" he asked; his own voice seemed distant somehow, as if he were underwater.

"Your mission is not complete. Get on your feet!" the voice screamed at him. Wolf's psyche flashed, and he was now looking up at his fallen companion. Darnel was wearing his military uniform with combat gear. He was firing from cover with his M4. Wolf could feel sand beneath his hands and body, the heat from the dry Afghan sun on his face. Cracks of bullets shattering concrete rang in his ears, as more and more guns sounded off. Darnel was in the heat of battle; he looked down at Wolf and grabbed his arm, shaking him violently. "Wolf! I need you! Stay with me! Follow my voice! Will! Come on, get on your feet, Marine!" Grabbing Wolf's hand, he placed his M&P into it, forcing Wolf to close his hand around the gun. "I need you!" he screamed once more.

Wolf lifted up his torso by pressing his left elbow into the ground, fighting the blinding pain, and took aim on one of the Taliban members. He couldn't lift his arm any higher than his shoulder due to the wounds the RPG explosion dealt on his body. He took aim on the terrorist soldier's left shin and fired. The man fell to his left knee. He went to aim his weapon at Wolf; before he could squeeze off a round, Wolf drilled him in the right shoulder with another bullet.

The Taliban soldier lay on his back, holding his left leg and right shoulder, screaming. The hot desert sand was replaced with cold floor tile; the hot sun was replaced by stark white ceilings illuminated by fluorescent lights. Wolf looked up to see Tyrone getting up from the floor, his left shin bleeding.

There was a large, five-foot window leading to another room behind him. The drug dealer pointed his gun towards Jessica, who was still laying on the floor. Wolf launched himself from the tile and drove his shoulder into Tyrone, sending both men crashing through the large window, into the other room. Tyrone held fast to the gun in his left hand and fired it off, narrowly missing Wolf's head. Wolf fought for control of the gun hand; Tyrone reversed position, taking Wolf to his back. As they rolled, Wolf slipped his left leg under the armpit of Tyrone and rolled out from underneath him, now with the drug dealer on his stomach and his left arm pinned behind his back, in the perfect seatbelt submission.

Tyrone squeezed off a couple more shots, all of them far from their mark. Wolf wrenched the man's arm forward, popping Tyrone's left shoulder out of socket and breaking his forearm across his calf. The drug dealer screamed in rage and pain, wrenching out from underneath Wolf's grip, clamoring back to his feet; Wolf struggled back to his feet as well. Tyrone grabbed a large shard of glass in his right hand and swung wildly, trying to cut Wolf. Calculating the times between swings, Wolf blocked his backswing and punched the man in the face, making him drop the shard of glass.

Like a bull, Tyrone charged Wolf and took him to the floor. Wolf pulled guard as Tyrone rained punches down on him wildly with his right hand. Making some space with his knee on Tyrone's chest, Wolf slipped his leg underneath Tyrone's right armpit and over his shoulder, trapping the shoulder so that his shin was across Tyrone's throat. Untying his boot, he wrapped the laces around the back of Tyrone's head, then hooked his right knee over his left foot, catching Tyrone in a Gogoplata choke. Arching his hips up and pulling down on the laces, Wolf held on as tight as he could as Tyrone's punches got weaker and weaker. After a few moments, the other man went limp, losing consciousness as the blood flow was cut off to his brain.

When he was sure that he was out, Wolf released the hold, letting his enemy fall to the floor. Both men lay motionless as Jessica called for help on a nearby intercom. Wolf began to fade in and out of reality; he could hear multiple voices shouting, a female above the rest, ordering people around. His body was lifted from the floor and placed on something firm. He felt people touching him and maneuver him. "We need him in surgery, now!" a voice shouted. Other voices began to join in, but he couldn't depict what they were saying. His world disappeared to blackness once more as his body slipped into that all too familiar void.

# Chapter 20

# The Redeemed

Wolf's eyes snapped open, revealing a clear sky painted with beautiful oranges, reds, pinks, and purples that reflected off the few clouds that were overhead. The ground he was on was firm and uneven, and it seemed to be shifting. He smelled the crisp sap of pine trees, carried by the chilling mountain air. He sat up slowly, his body feeling heavy but otherwise healthy. Wolf saw that he was sitting on a dock that was being rocked by the wind on a lake. Snow topped mountains surrounded him on every side, their silhouettes painted by the bright orange sun setting on the horizon.

"Beautiful, isn't it?" a voice said behind him. Wolf turned his body toward the voice and sprang to his feet, ready for anything. Darnel sat on a wood bench built onto the dock; he was wearing combat boots, military-issued cargo pants, and a white t-shirt, his dog tags hanging close to his chest. A beautiful acoustic guitar sat next to him.

Wolf's eyes grew wide. "Darnel?" he asked.

The other man smiled at him, "In the flesh. Well, sort of," he chuckled.

"You look good, little brother."

Wolf raised his eyebrow at him, "As do you."

Darnel smiled; pulling out a pocket knife, he began to cut into a green apple. He always ate his apples that way, never biting into them. He ate the slice he had cut off and gestured towards Wolf with the blade. "You should look into the water at your reflection," he said in between munches on the apple slice.

Panic struck Wolf's heart. "You know I can't…"

Darnel cut another slice of the apple and bit into it, "It's not that you can't, my friend, it's that you won't. You know those scars don't define you as a monster; they define you as a warrior: a fierce one at that."

Wolf looked away from his friend. "They are a constant reminder of the animal that I am," Wolf said, his voice filled with shame. A tear began to form in his eye, but he wiped it away before his brother could see it.

Darnel nodded and took another slice out of his apple. This time he held it on the blade. "Wolf, look at me," he said. Wolf kept his eyes trained on the hardwood deck beneath his feet. "William, please," his friend pleaded.

Wolf lifted his eyes toward him and met his gaze. Darnel picked the slice off the blade and lifted it up for Wolf to see, "What do you make of this apple slice?" he asked.

Wolf shrugged. "It is a piece of the apple," Wolf answered.

Darnel smiled. "Correct," he said. "Would you agree that this slice is still a part of the apple itself?" Wolf nodded his head, unsure as to where his friend was going with this. "This piece is a scarred remnant from the apple it once inhabited. Is that correct?" Darnel continued.

"I guess so," Wolf responded.

"So, in a sense, this apple slice is much like your heart. It was once valiant: strong. You would dive headlong into battle, whether it was after the heart of a woman or for the honor of your country. You were a man people enjoyed to be around because all you wanted to do was serve others before yourself. Then life took a piece of that heart from you when you were scarred by that explosion. You lost your fiancé, your home, your car, your reason to live.

"When I found you in that alleyway, I saw your heart was still valiant. Yes, you nearly killed that man, but the look in your eyes told me that was not what you had become. Brother, that man in the alleyway that stood there with a bloody knife in his hand, is not who you are, it never was. You are the greatest man that I have ever known."

Tears began to flow down Wolf's face. "I'm not a man, Darnel. I killed those people. I have killed so many people and hurt so many more. These scars physically show the monster I am inside."

"Yet you hide from them," Darnel countered. "You won't look at yourself in the mirror because it's so much easier to lie to yourself if you aren't staring into your own eyes. A man is not defined by his actions but by who he truly is. Any truly bad man could do worldly good, yet his heart is soiled with wickedness and deception. Your heart is that of a warrior. Do you remember the conversation that you had with Jessica in our living room?" Darnel asked.

Wolf thought for a second. "Do you mean, what she said about that 'David' guy?" he asked.

Darnel smiled. "That would be the one," he said. "The story of David is a wild one. There was a woman by the name of Bathsheba who was bathing on her rooftop. David was on his rooftop as well and just happened to see her naked. He was so filled with lust that he couldn't stop thinking about her, so he sent for her and had her come to his home so that he could sleep with her. Now, the real kicker is that she was married. Her husband was Uriah, the Hittite, one of David's soldiers, a very valuable one at that. He was loyal, he was valiant, and he was a fierce warrior. David knew very well that she was a married woman, but he did it anyway. Back in the day, they didn't have birth control, so she got pregnant. She told David as soon as she found out, so he sent a message to his servant Joab to send Uriah home from the war.

"When Uriah arrived, David tried to get him to go home and sleep with his wife. But as faithful and as loyal of a soldier Uriah was, he could only think of the battle and his brothers in arms. Uriah slept on David's doorstep instead of going home. The next night, David got him drunk and tried to get him to go home and sleep with his wife, but Uriah would not do it. This threw a wrench in David's plan, so he wrote a letter for his servant Joab to have Uriah at the frontline during a battle that he knew would be a deadly one. Once the battle commenced, he would have the other men step back and let Uriah die."

Wolf raised his eyebrow. "Wow," he said.

Darnel nodded, "That's not even the worst part; he gave the letter to Uriah and had him take his own death warrant to Joab. He was so loyal that he did not open the letter and did as David had instructed, bringing it straight to Joab. The order was carried out and Uriah was slaughtered. After Uriah was confirmed dead, David took Bathsheba as his wife so that the child she had was accepted. So basically, David was an adulterer, a liar, and a murderer. He thought he had gotten away with it, but a year later his evil deeds were brought to life by a man named Nathan. David instantly begged for forgiveness from the Lord, saying that he had sinned against God and God alone.

"Now, the Lord forgave him. He even called him a man after His own heart. Yes, his deeds were terrible, and there was a lot more to David's life that was just as terrible: his son sexually assaulted his daughter, and then his other son murdered his own half-brother for the honor of his sister, because David did nothing about it. God still called him a man after His own heart. Because David had a servant's heart, he truly hated the actions he had done, because he knew that they were the actions of a monster. But that didn't define who he was.

"You have a servant's heart William: you always have. Yes, you have made mistakes. Yes, you have done terrible things, but you are still a great man by who you truly are. Why do you think I called you Wolf all those years ago and continued to up until we had to depart?"

Wolf shifted his feet, "Because I'm an animal?"

Darnel shook his head, "No." He stood up and placed his left hand on Wolf's shoulder and his right hand on the back of Wolf's head. He stared deep into the other man's eyes, "Because you are a natural-born leader. It's time to take up your sword, brother. Become the man I have always known you to be: a man after God's own heart."

Wolf burst out into tears and Darnel pulled him into his shoulder, letting him cry it out. "I will always love you like a brother and I am excited to see you grow into the man that you were meant to be."

He then stepped away from Wolf, walked over to the guitar, and began strumming a soft tune: the all too familiar riff of their favorite song. "What do you say, brother," Darnel inquired, "one last time?"

Wolf smiled through his tears and nodded his head, "I'd love to, my brother."

Darnel smiled and began singing their favorite song, his voice soft and soulful. Wolf joined in, their voices uniting in perfect harmony. Both men belted out the song together, feeling every emotion and recalling every memory they shared with this one song. They continued to sing together all the way through until Darnel strummed the last chord. He smiled once more at Wolf as tears rolled down his cheeks. Wolf had tears in his own eyes, knowing that the song now had a new meaning to both men: one of hope and deliverance from fallen kingdoms they once held.

"So," Wolf said, "you find Delilah yet?"

Darnel smiled, "I found her."

Wolf smiled back, "Good. When do I get to meet her?"

Darnel set the guitar back against the bench, "When it's your time to come home. In the meantime, my house was always meant to be a home. You should invest into making it one." He hugged his best friend close, "God bless, my brother. Stay close to Jessica; she's a keeper."

Wolf laughed, "I will keep that in mind."

Darnel smiled, "Goodbye for now, brother."

Wolf nodded his head and then Darnel released him. The mountains began to blur, the painted sky faded to black, and the crisp air no longer kissed Wolf's cheeks. His best friend, his brother, was gone once more. Only still darkness flooded his mind's eye.

# Chapter 21

# The Found

June 10th, 2013, 12:30 p.m. Wolf woke up in a very clean room; he was lying in a soft bed. He went to move his hand up to wipe his eyes, but his wrist was stopped short. Looking down at his arm, he noticed shiny metal handcuffs were attached to his left wrist and the handle of the bed.

"Good to see you finally awake, Mr. Jackson," a female voice said. Wolf looked over to see the familiar face of Detective Kate Westbrooke, sitting in a chair in the room, staring at him.

"Good morning to you, too. Mind taking these off?" Wolf asked.

She shrugged, "I would say you are under arrest, but that's not true." Then she stood up, walked over to his chained wrists, and set him free. "You attacked the doctor a couple times when you were under. We had to restrain you so you wouldn't rip out your stitches." She stood at the foot of his bed. "I just thought that you would like to know that due to evidence and some confessions from witnesses, we have enough to lock Tyrone away for Darnel's murder as well as a few other unsolved murders. He used that SUV for a lot of bad hits, apparently. Also, having both Bishop and Damien flip on him helped a lot, too."

Wolf nodded his head, "That's great news."

She smiled at him, "Well, I owe it to you for taking him alive. Better to make him suffer for his crimes."

Silence filled the room. Wolf finally broke the long pause, "So, what happens now, Kate?"

She shrugged. "Well, seeing that you were shot in the chest four times, stabbed twice, shot in both shoulders, your left bicep, and your left leg, I can't hire you as a detective anytime soon," she said.

The door opened and Jess walked hesitantly into the room. "Sorry... I heard he was awake..."

The other woman smiled at her familiar face, "No worries, Jess. I was just telling Will the good news."

"I hope they take down his entire organization," Jess replied.

"We will. The process has already begun. Will made sure of that," she said, looking over at Wolf. "Heal up so I can hire you," she said, and then excused herself from the room so Jess and Will could be alone.

Wolf looked over at Jessica, "Is it too late to reschedule our date?" he asked.

She beamed at him; the left side of her face was a little swollen from where Tyrone struck her, but other than that, she was as beautiful as always. Still dressed in her scrubs, she walked over to the bed with her hands behind her back. "Why would we reschedule when we can have it now?" she asked, then placed a take-home container on the little table that was over his lap. She opened it to reveal steak and eggs.

Wolf smiled at her and they spent the rest of the afternoon together, getting to know one another until both fell asleep, him in the bed and her in the chair next to him. Wolf woke up to the sound of the door opening: it was Matt. He smiled at Wolf as he walked in. Wolf put a finger to his lips but motioned for him to sit in another chair right next to him. Matt sat down and leaned close.

"I heard you got him," he said in a hushed tone.

Wolf smiled and nodded, "He is going to pay for everything he has done. Damien too."

"Praise God," he said with a smile. "How you holding up?"

Wolf looked at him and smiled, "I saw Darnel."

Matt's eyes widened, "What? How?"

Wolf told him about the dock and his meeting with Darnel. Matt's eyes were tearing up and he kept saying, "Praise God," in absolute awe.

Wolf nodded his head and smiled, "Yeah it was truly amazing. I want what he had, Matt."

The pastor raised his eyebrows at him. "Yeah?" he asked.

Wolf nodded, "I want what you have, too. Teach me how to love Jesus."

Matt beamed, "Ask Him to redeem you. Pray from the heart."

Wolf nodded, "Okay, here goes nothing…" He took a breath. "Lord… I uh… I never really prayed before… but, if You could take one marine, maybe You have room for another… I have made many mistakes… but I want to be someone else, something else… I want what Darnel had before he was taken from this world. I want the love and the peace he had in his heart. If You could redeem him… I want to know if, maybe You could make beauty from these ashes. Forgive me, renew me… um, amen. I think that's how I'm supposed to end this. Amen?"

A tear trickled down his cheek; with a blink he let it fall off his chin. Matt had tears in his eyes as well. "Amen," he said.

Jessica's hand squeezed Wolf's; he looked over to see tears in her eyes, too. "Amen," she said, and kissed his hand.

Wolf smiled at both of them. "Now what?" he asked, and all three laughed.

Matt asked to pray over Wolf. He agreed. Bowing his head, he began, "Father, bless this newly adopted son that has joined the ranks of Your Kingdom. May he see You in every aspect of his life from this day forward. Bless him and show him Your grace with everything in his life. Amen." He smiled at Wolf and embraced him. Both visitors left shortly after that. Jess had a shift the next morning and Matt had to help his wife with the boys.

Every day for the next three weeks, Jessica would come in before and after her shift, with some sort of food and date planned. They talked about their pasts and their interests. She taught him scripture and bought him a Bible. Wolf discovered that she was a gymnast and cheerleader in high school. Her favorite snack was chocolate and favorite food was green apples with peanut butter. They talked about music, how they grew up, marriage, and if they wanted kids. Wolf knew that this girl was special and he anxiously waited every day for her to come in to visit him.

# Chapter 22

# The Honored

June 30th, 2013, 12:00 p.m. Jessica entered the room. She was wearing a modest, yet elegant, black dress that hugged her figure just right. Her hair was pulled back underneath a black hat with lace that cascaded over her face. She had a large suit bag over her shoulder that she was holding by the hanger with her fingertips. Wolf cocked his good eyebrow at her. She placed the bag across his legs and put her hands on his face. "Are you ready to get out of here?" she asked, looking at him with those piercingly loving eyes.

"Darnel's funeral?" he asked.

She nodded, choking back tears, then unzipped the bag, revealing his dress blues. He raised his good eyebrow once more at her. "I figured you'd want to honor Darnel by wearing it at his funeral."

A tear formed in his eye. "Thank you," he managed to choke out.

She smiled, "You're welcome. I'm going to call in a male orderly to help get you dressed. See you soon." She leaned over and kissed him gently on the cheek, then walked out of the room. A male orderly walked in moments after she had left and began to undo all the wiring and tubes that were attached to him so he could get dressed.

The man was in his mid-twenties; he seemed fit enough to carry Wolf's weight. He reached his hand out to Wolf and said, "Hi, my name is John."

Wolf took his hand, "Will. Nice to meet you."

The other man nodded his head and smiled, "Well, I've been ordered by the big boss, Jess, to get you into your dress blues. Let's start with your pants, alright?"

"Can I use the bathroom first?" Wolf asked. The man nodded and helped him to the bathroom.

Wolf now stood in front of the bathroom mirror, shirtless, gripping both sides of the sink. "Alright Wolf, just look. You can look. You are redeemed…" he told himself, over and over again.

Finally, he lifted his head. A feeling of peace washed over his body. He was now staring into the face of a man that had been beaten and scarred but yet here he stood. He saw the gauze on his chest, and he began to pull them off, revealing the new stitches on his chest. But instead of hurting, he was overwhelmed with a sense of peace, like a gladiator that just won his freedom. For the first time in what seemed like forever, he saw himself smile back at him in the mirror.

He opened the door and let John back in. John put new dressings on Wolf's stitches and helped him get his dress blues on. Once he was ready to go, Jessica walked back in the room, pushing a wheelchair in front of her and smiling at him. "You look great," she said, and then her face sank. "I just wish he could have been here with us."

Wolf nodded his head and sat down in the wheelchair, unable to find his voice to comfort her. She wheeled him out of the room, into the elevator and then out of the hospital. She walked over to the Chevelle that had been parked in a staff parking spot. Wolf looked at her and raised his good eyebrow. "I couldn't resist… I hope you don't mind," she said, evidently unsure how he would react.

He chuckled and shook his head, then grabbed her hand to assure her that it was okay. She pushed him over to the passenger door and helped him into the seat, buckling him in. Then she put the wheelchair in the trunk and got in the driver seat. She turned the key and the engine roared to life. She expertly pulled out of the parking lot and drove down the road, heading straight for the church.

June 30th, 2013, 2:45 p.m. Wolf and Jessica arrived in front of the church; multiple cars had already filled most of the parking lot. Jessica got out of the car and retrieved the wheelchair from the trunk. She wheeled it close to Wolf's door and helped him out of the passenger seat of the car and into the wheelchair. She paused and looked into Wolf's eyes. "Are you ready for this?" she asked, concern in her eyes.

Wolf reached up and held her cheek in his hand, "How could anyone be ready to say goodbye to someone they love?" he asked.

She nodded her head and kissed his hand, then stepped behind him and pushed him towards the church doors. A couple of men were at the doors and opened them so the two could get inside with no troubles. Both thanked the gentlemen and continued into the sanctuary. It was packed with people. Flowers were all over the stage as well as a picture of Darnel in his service uniform. There was a guitar on a stand next to the photos: Darnel's favorite acoustic. A slideshow of pictures of Darnel played above the stage. The pictures consisted of him at the church playing his guitar, smiling, and socializing with people. The slideshow was playing music that Wolf did not recognize. However, the lyrics touched his heart in a very intimate way. It was a song of pure unconditional love, a story of God meeting whomever He called *child*, wherever they may be, promising to remain with them, even when circumstance hinders their sight of Him. He would always be there to pick them back up to their feet. Tears formed in Wolf's eyes as he began to get lost in the beautiful melody, knowing that God was speaking to him through it.

Wolf leaned back slightly and asked Jessica who the song was sung by. She smiled and leaned down so she could whisper in his ear, "Tenth Avenue North. It was Darnel's favorite."

Wolf whispered back into her ear, "I can see why. It is beautiful."
She smiled and continued to push him up to the front row and park his
wheelchair in the middle of the aisle, just left of the pew. Jess sat right
next to him. Wolf heard a gruff bark; he looked over to his right to see
Beef sprinting at him as fast as his little, fat legs could carry him. He
reached his master's feet and stood up on his hind legs, wagging his
whole rear end in excitement, and snorting wildly.

Wolf chuckled. "It's good to see you too buddy," he said, as he
reached down and scratched the fat rolls on his head. Jessica scooped
the hefty white dog off the floor and into her lap so that he could get
affection by both his master and her. Beef loved every second of it,
shaking his leg in appreciation.

Matt was off to the left talking to somebody, but as soon as he saw
Wolf, he excused himself from the conversation and walked over to
him. He smiled at him; it was a sad smile but a loving one nonetheless.
"You're looking better, brother; glad to see you got out of that bed
finally," he said.

Wolf nodded his head, "I feel like I had some help to accomplish
that. Maybe those prayers of yours were exactly what I needed."

Matt smiled, "Glad to hear it. I want to personally thank you once
again for saving my family." The young pastor reached out his hand
and Wolf took it.

"You're welcome," Wolf replied. "But it is I who should be
thanking you, Matt, for saving mine."

The young pastor smiled, "It was my pleasure." With that, the
pastor walked to the center of the aisle and stood before the mass of
people. The music cut out and Matt picked up a microphone from one
of the altars. "Hello everyone; thank you for being here today.
Unfortunately, it is a day that we say goodbye to a man that so many
of us had called a friend and cherished loved one. Darnel was a real
man: he was tough, he was smart, he was loyal, and he was

compassionate. When I first met him, he had beat up one of the drug dealers that used to plague these streets out front of this very church. The crazy thing was, he was drunk when he did it. Soon he began playing bodyguard in front of the church, keeping all the violence and drugs away from our youth.

"The first three months we knew each other, he was a tough nut to crack. He was quiet: stoic like a statue. I thought that I had made a terrible mistake by inviting him to our men's groups on Thursday nights, but then I really got to know him for who he was. When I first heard him play his guitar and sing on this very stage, I saw him in a brand-new light. Instead of viewing him as a man hardened by war, I found just the opposite. I saw a man so wounded by war that he had to guard himself. Although, when he opened up, his emotions and compassion for other people were so deeply embedded in him that he was one of the most incredible people I ever got the privilege to know." The pastor began to tear up. He cleared his throat and apologized to the crowd.

He looked over at Wolf and reached his hand out towards him, "However, whatever I say could never give justice to just what caliber of man Darnel was. His best friend, Lieutenant William Jackson is here today, and I would love it if he could come up here and truly express what an amazing individual Darnel was. Will?" he said, then he walked over and helped Wolf to the stage in his wheelchair. He handed Wolf the microphone and took a seat with his family.

Wolf sat before the crowd, fighting back the tears. Clearing his throat, he began. "Darnel and I met when I joined the military. He was my platoon commander, and well, we were inseparable ever since. He saved my life countless times, and I tried to return the favor as much as possible. I didn't have any family back then, but he became my family. Even after the war, he continued to save my life. He took me in when I had nowhere else to go, gave me a reason to live.

"He was an honest man; he told you exactly what he was thinking, even if you didn't ask his opinion." He chuckled after that and shook his head. "Darnel was more than a great friend; he was also an outstanding human being. He would give his life at the drop of a hat for another person. He was compassionate, he was strong, and he was one of the most trust-worthy people I have ever known. More than that, he was the greatest man I had ever known. I wish he could be here with us, but I know he's in a better place. I wish he would have brought me here so I could meet all of you people under better circumstances... Even in his death, he continues to save my life. He was my best friend, my hero, but most of all, he was my brother."

Wolf set the microphone down on the altar and then turned his chair, applied the brakes, and stood up. He turned towards his fallen comrade, lying in his coffin, and saluted him. Darnel seemed like he was sleeping; he was in his service uniform, a fit burial for a soldier of his caliber. "I love you brother. Thank you, for everything." He then limped as he struggled to walk. He picked up the guitar on a stand next to the coffin. "If you guys don't mind, I would love to play a song that he and I used to sing with each other. I know he would want it played..." Everyone nodded in approval; he began to strum the opening chords. Taking in a deep breath, he began to let the words from their favorite song fill the sanctuary.

His voice shook as he recalled the small time he spent with Darnel on the dock. Images of the scars on his body, once strongholds he claimed as his kingdom, now ashes as the inner beauty shown through. His kingdom, this worldly empire he carried, was no longer one of pain and charred rubble, but one of beauty rising from the ashes. For the first time Wolf could recall, he was free.

Wolf ended the final verse and broke down sobbing, falling into his wheelchair. Jessica was quickly at his side to wheel him back to where they were sitting. Every eye in the house flowed with tears. Matt closed out the ceremony with a prayer. People walked up the aisle and paid their respects to Darnel, saying their final goodbyes.

Thirty minutes later, Wolf and Jessica were at the cemetery where Darnel was being rolled in on a horse-drawn carriage by military personnel, all were wearing their service uniforms and carrying rifles. An American flag was draped across his coffin. They carried Darnel to his final resting place while a trumpet played the ceremonial burial music. They set him on the machine that would lower him into the earth. The twenty-one men in uniform raised their rifles and at their commander's instruction, they fired in unison, performing the 21 gun salute. Then four men pulled the flag off the coffin, pulling it taught, about chest high, and began folding it tightly into a triangular shape. The man that had finished the folding, carried it over to Wolf, who sat in his wheelchair next to Jessica. The marine placed the flag into Wolf's hands and saluted him. Wolf slowly and painfully stood to his feet to salute the marine right back.

Helping him back into his chair, the marine whispered a blessing into Wolf's good ear, and an apology for his loss. Then he rejoined his rank and marched away as people began filing forward to pay their respects. Shortly after, Wolf and Jessica were the only ones remaining. The groundskeepers powered on the machine and lowered the coffin into the earth. Jessica got out of her chair and helped Wolf back to the car where Beef waited for them, his tail wagging excitedly at his master's return. Wolf scratched his head and helped him into the back seat of the Chevelle. With help from Jessica, he lowered himself into his seat and buckled up. Jess put the wheelchair into the trunk and then climbed into the driver seat and left the cemetery.

# Chapter 23

# The Life Given

June 5th, 2018, 8:00 a.m. Wolf sat with his legs crossed, on the floor of his living room. He was wearing pajama pants and had no shirt on. The scars from the five bullets Tyron had shot into his chest, as well as the burn scars from the RPG shell that almost killed him in Afghanistan, were revealed for anyone that happened to walk into the room to see. No longer did he believe them to be his curse, but simply scars. Nothing more, nothing less. They no longer defined him as a monster, but refined him as a man.

He leaned his back up against the couch and stroked the top of Beef's head at his side. A beaten up, black, leather-bound Bible lay open on his lap to 1 Corinthians chapter 13; he was deep into it, studying as much as he could, absorbing it in like a sponge. A small, dark-toned hand blotted out the part of the page he was reading and he looked up to see a black baby boy, no more than about eight months old, with bright blue eyes smiling up at him behind his pacifier. His little black afro billowed out in an untamed mess. He was wearing bright blue footie pajamas. He reached up towards Wolf's face and formed a very muffled, "Da-da," through his pacifier.

Wolf smiled at him, "Good morning, Darnel. Do you want to read with Daddy?"

The little boy just stared at him with those bright blue eyes, that smile still on his face. Wolf scooped him up and set him in his lap with the Bible held out in front of both of them. "Alright Son, this is First Corinthians, chapter thirteen, verses four through thirteen:

'Love is patient and kind; love does not envy or boast; it is not arrogant or rude. It does not insist on its own way; it is not irritable or resentful; it does not rejoice at wrongdoing, but rejoices with the truth. Love bears all things, believes all things, hopes all things, endures all things.

Love never ends. As for prophecies, they will pass away; as for tongues, they will cease; as for knowledge, it will pass away. For we know in part and we prophesy in part, but when the perfect comes, the partial will pass away.

When I was a child, I spoke like a child, I thought like a child, I reasoned like a child. When I became a man, I gave up childish ways. For now we see in a mirror dimly, but then face to face. Now I know in part; then I shall know fully, even as I have been fully known.

So now faith, hope, and love abide, these three; but the greatest of these is love.'"

He kissed the top of the little boy's head and placed the Bible on the couch behind him. Then, he picked up his son so that they could see each other face to face. He sighed and smiled at the beautiful boy he held in his hands. "Son, five years ago today, your Daddy lost his best friend. His name was Darnel; that's who you are named after. He was the greatest man that I have ever known." He paused as he choked down his emotions. "I named you after him because I know that one day, when you become a man, you will take up his name with honor and people will know that where you walk, our Father is right next to you." The little boy giggled and he kissed him on his little, chubby cheeks.

"If I were to teach you anything, Son, let it be this: keep your faith always in the Lord, because He will never leave you or forsake you. Keep the hope that one day you too will find the peace and happiness that I have found through God and with your beautiful mother. But most of all, love as much as you can. God has big plans for you, my son; I see it even now at such a young age. Wherever life takes you, show the love of the Father: be selfless, be patient, be kind, be compassionate, be merciful, be loyal, and most of all, be ready to lay down your life for another. Do these things, my son, and you will truly become the greatest man that I have ever known. I look forward to that day with all the love and anticipation I have in my heart." The baby stared at him and put his tiny, soft hands on his daddy's face. Wolf pulled him in and nibbled on his little cheeks, making the young boy giggle.

"I think he has a pretty good shot," a female voice behind him exclaimed softly. He turned around to see Jessica standing next to the couch behind him. "His Daddy is a man after God's own heart," she said with a loving wink. Her hair was matted and she didn't have on any make-up, but she still took his breath away. She was wearing light blue, plaid pajama pants with a white t-shirt.

He smiled and wondered how he could ever have won this beautifully perfect woman over. She slid to the floor next to him and snuggled up close to his arm, with Beef lying down in between their hips. She tickled the little baby's belly and he giggled. "Hello, my handsome young man," she cooed at the little baby boy. She patted Wolf on the leg, rubbing it gently with her left hand. He smiled at her when he once again caught her admiring the rose gold ring with a pear-shaped ruby and diamond halo on her finger.

"Still admiring that ring, I see," he chided at her.

She smiled, "Maybe I just love the man I married."

He chuckled. "Three years later and she still has the stars in her eyes," he said to the baby boy, winking at him. The little baby smiled at him behind the pacifier, noticing that he was getting attention once more.

Jessica kissed Wolf tenderly on the cheek and then patted his leg, "We have to get ready for church. Worship leader can't be late. Matt will have your head," she teased.

Wolf chuckled. "Hey, you laugh, but you didn't see what the MVP of baseball for Catholic schoolboys can do with a bat," he said with a wink. She laughed that wonderful laugh he so much enjoyed.

"Does Jace need us to unlock the church for him?" she asked.

Wolf smiled as he remembered the young kid lost in a world of drugs and violence, who had once held a shotgun to his chest so many years ago. The young kid later showed up at the church, searching for Wolf, to thank him once more. Next thing Wolf knew, he was mentoring the young man. He was amazed at how much had changed since that time: Wolf and Jess got married; he became a cop for a couple years before becoming a homicide detective, with Kate as his immediate supervisor; he even became the worship leader at the church. From nothing to everything. Remembering his wife asked a question, he snapped back into the now and responded, "No, I texted him this morning, he's already at the church. He carpooled with Matt so the pastor's wife could sleep in."

She smiled, "Sounds good to me." She kissed him tenderly. "But we really do have to get ready."

He took another look at her natural beauty, smiling. He stood up with the baby in his left arm and then helped lift his wife off his floor with his right hand. Once she was on her feet, he kissed her softly. "Do you want me to get Darnel ready so you can get in the shower real quick?" he asked.

She shook her head, "No thank you. You got him fed and changed his diaper this morning, plus I showered last night."

Wolf kissed her forehead and handed the baby off to her, then went and took a shower. Twenty minutes later, he stood in the front room in nice dress pants with a royal blue dress shirt, still trying to button up the cuffs. He looked up at the American flag in a triangular prism frame with a glass face. He looked at it long and hard, Darnel's dog tags were pressed up against the glass. Wolf wiped a tear and saluted the flag. Jessica came up behind him and wrapped her hand around his waist. "He'd be proud of you," she said.

He patted her hand and turned to embrace her. She was now in a simple white dress with a floral design. Wolf couldn't help but stare at her; she was gorgeous. He scooped his Bible off the couch and then snagged the diaper bag and baby from her. She handed him a green apple which he bit into, holding it firmly in his teeth, winking at her. Then he headed out to his truck, Beef right behind him. He set the diaper bag on the back floorboard and put the baby in his car seat. Then he lifted Beef into the front so that he could sit in the middle of the bench. He grabbed the apple from his mouth, biting out a chunk, and began eating it. Jessica got into the front passenger seat; she was holding a dozen white roses on her lap. Wolf climbed into the driver seat and started the vehicle.

He drove down the road in the hot Denver air. His mind was swimming with emotions and memories of his best friend as he made his way across town. He was biting into his apple, remaining completely silent. Jessica sensed his emotional state and let him stay in silence. Finally, he had reached his destination, pulling into the cemetery where his brother had been buried. He got as close to the grave as he could by car and put the big Ford F150 into park, leaving the key in the ignition. He looked over to Jessica and she handed him the bundle of roses. "Take your time; we'll be here," she said. Wolf nodded his thanks and climbed out of the truck.

He walked twenty or so yards, past the graves of loved ones people had lost. All had served their country; whether they died at war or at home, this is where they were buried. His pace slowed as he reached his best friend's final resting place. There was a white cross on his burial site. It read: *Lieutenant Darnel Uriah Jones; Born October 29th, 1977; Died June 5th, 2013; One of the greatest men this world has ever known.*

Wolf had it inscribed himself. Standing there in the hot sun, he stared at the white stone cross. He took in a deep breath, calming his emotions. "Hey Darnel, it's me. Jess and little Darnel are doing great, man, he's getting so big. I wish you were here to enjoy them as my family with me, brother, but I know that you are with the Father and much happier than you could ever be here. I think every day about the time you and I spent on that dock in the mountains; whether it was a vision or just a dream, it changed my life. I sought out God and found Him... He has given me a peace that I have never known before. He's given me the most amazing wife and beautiful son, with another miracle on the way. Even in death, you had my back. I hope I can repay that to you by becoming the man that you believed I could be."

Tears flowed hot down his cheeks, "I really wish you were here with me, brother. But I am so proud of the man you were when you died. You went out defending the innocent; classic Darnel..." he cleared his throat, trying to get a hold of his emotions. "I will never forget all that you did for me and I am going to raise my son to be a God-honoring man, just like you. Thank you for everything you did for me in life. I don't know if I ever truly thanked you for all that you had done. I love you, my brother... God bless." He placed the flowers on the grave and shoved his hands in his pockets. He walked slowly back to his truck where his family waited for him.

He took a deep breath, wiped his tears, and then climbed into the driver seat of his truck. Beef *gruffed* a greeting to his master and Wolf scratched his head. Jessica looked at him with deep compassion in her eyes. "Are you okay?" she asked.

Wolf sniffed back a sob, clearing his throat as he wiped away the tears in his eyes. "Yeah... just..." his voice trailed off.

Jessica grabbed his hand; he looked over and saw her staring into his eyes with so much compassion. "I know, I miss him too," she said, as she reached up and wiped the tears from his eyes.

Wolf nuzzled her hand on his face. "I love you," he said.

"I love you too," she said.

He leaned over and kissed her cheek. Putting the truck in gear, he pulled out of the cemetery and began driving down the road. Jessica reached over to the stereo and flipped it on. A familiar song played through the speakers and Wolf couldn't help but smile through his tears as his and his brother's redemption song, sung by Tenth Avenue North, filled the cab of the truck. The song pierced his heart just as it had done the first time he heard it at Darnel's funeral service. He let the music carry his emotions away as he rumbled down the road. He felt the presence of the Lord fill the cab of the truck and was grateful for the family that he had now been given, knowing that he now had a hope and a promise for the future.

Wolf Jackson

Jordan Flowers is available for interviews and personal appearances. For more information contact:

Jordan Flowers
C/O Advantage Books
P.O. Box 160847
Altamonte Springs, FL 32716
info@advbooks.com

To purchase additional copies of this book visit our bookstore website at: www.advbookstore.com

Longwood, Florida, USA
"we bring dreams to life"™
www.advbookstore.com

CPSIA information can be obtained
at www.ICGtesting.com
Printed in the USA
LVHW080429160422
716375LV00020B/518